15 MINUTES

15 MINUTES

A novel by
Gary Goldstein

Based on the screenplay
by John Herzfeld

AN ONYX BOOK

ONYX
Published by New American Library, a division of
Penguin Putnam Inc., 375 Hudson Street,
New York, New York 10014, U.S.A.
Penguin Books Ltd, 27 Wrights Lane,
London W8 5TZ, England
Penguin Books Australia Ltd, Ringwood,
Victoria, Australia
Penguin Books Canada Ltd, 10 Alcorn Avenue,
Toronto, Ontario, Canada M4V 3B2
Penguin Books (N.Z.) Ltd, 182–190 Wairau Road,
Auckland 10, New Zealand

Penguin Books Ltd, Registered Offices:
Harmondsworth, Middlesex, England

First published by Onyx, an imprint of New American Library,
a division of Penguin Putnam Inc.

First Printing, January 2001
10   9   8   7   6   5   4   3   2   1

ONE

Czech Airlines Flight 555 left Prague, in the Czech Republic, at ten p.m., a nonstop flight to New York's Kennedy Airport. Aboard the Boeing 747, in seats 28B and 28C sat two men. On a serving tray, the occupant of 28B was counting Czech currency. Also on the serving tray were three miniature vodka bottles, the kind served on airplanes, and a disposable camera. The money didn't amount to much—maybe fifty dollars American at the exchange counter, but the man in 28B wasn't worried. Some people in New York City owed him money, and he aimed to get it one way or the other.

Turning his attention away from the money, the man in 28B reached into his breast pocket and pulled out two passports. One belonged to an Emil Slovak; the other belonged to one Oleg Razgul. He passed Oleg Razgul's passport to the man next to him with the instructions, spoken in Czech: "Just do what I do. Say the same thing I say. Don't open your mouth."

The man in 28C replied, also in Czech, "Okay."

They were going to America, land of opportunity, where the streets were paved with gold. The party was about to begin.

It was called *Top Story* and it was, at that very moment, the highest-rated tabloid television show on any network. The highbrow critics decried it as "trash TV," but they were only a tiny minority. The public loved *Top Story*; it was a ratings smash in the seven-to-eight p.m. time slot it had occupied for the past five years. Most of the show's success was the result of one man—*Top Story's* host, Robert Hawkins. A tireless newshound, Hawkins put Geraldo and the rest of those prime-time bums to shame. You wanted O.J., Lorena Bobbitt, Amy Fisher and Joey Buttafuco, Jeffrey Dahmer or the serial killer *du jour*, you tuned into *Top Story*.

Never one to bask in his own success, Robert Hawkins chased the hot story of the hour with the determination of a ravenous pit bull. When a mother and son team of con artists murdered an eighty-two-year-old lady on the Upper East Side to gain possession of her elegant town house—estimated worth a cool six million dollars—Hawkins was granted the first jailhouse interview. When three cops from the 130th Precinct pumped twenty bullets into an unarmed immigrant in a Bronx tenement in a case of mistaken identity, Hawkins was the first to telecast the scenes of the immigrant's grieving parents. Even the competition grudgingly admitted that Robert Hawkins was the best in the tabloid TV business. Robert Hawkins always brought home the ratings bacon.

Today, however, Robert Hawkins was not a particularly happy man. Success always demanded more success, and while Hawkins was always up to the task, the network top brass had been on his case lately. Something about *Top Story* being a shade on the sleazy side. (Not that the pecker-head execs complained much when the ad revenue dollars poured in, of course.) As a result, Robert Hawkins found himself waging a one-man war to grab the stories that guaranteed to keep *Top Story* at the top of the ratings.

Top Story occupied one of the higher floors—as befit its status as a smash—in a high-rise building at Forty-Fifth and Broadway. Inside the office of Cassandra Adams, *Top Story*'s senior producer, Robert Hawkins paced angrily back and forth, ignoring the spectacular view of Times Square from the floor-to-ceiling windows.

"Bullshit!" Hawkins complained to Cassandra Adams, his face beet red. "Abandoned baby in Times Square, come on! It's too fucking soft. It won't work and we won't get the numbers."

Cassandra turned in her swivel chair and faced Hawkins. She was thirty-five, smart, tough as nails, and extremely beautiful and sexy to boot. She said impatiently, "What are you suggesting, Robert—that we manufacture bad news?"

"That's what they tune us in for," he said. "We're a tabloid show—they tune us in for the rough stuff."

Hawkins was a little over six feet tall, with a seriously receding hairline and slight bulldog jaw. He was earnest and compassionate and funny, depending on the interviewee, be he or she an ax murderer or some colorful Joe Six-pack from Brooklyn. America loved him.

"Look," Cassandra replied, "the network's up my pretty little ass to make a change. Every lobbyist, every soccer mom and politician is screaming about violence in prime time. We've got to broaden the format."

Hawkins was angry and flustered. And he was rarely if ever flustered. He said, "Okay, you broaden the format. In the end, the story they'll run is the one with the *juice*. They want ratings just as much as I do." He put his hands flat on Cassandra's desk, looked her square in the eye, and announced, "If it *bleeds*, it *leads*!"

Maggie Henderson, Hawkins's assistant, entered Cassandra's office with a knock. She was followed by her mousy assistant, whose name Hawkins had never bothered to learn.

Hawkins said to Maggie, "What have you got?"

Thinking the boss would be pleased, Maggie said proudly, "I've got a ride-along with Eddie Flemming."

Hawkins exploded. "Fuck! Again?"

Hoping to mollify him, Maggie's assistant bravely held up the cover of a magazine and said, "He's on the cover of *People* this week."

"No, no, no—listen: He is not new." Hawkins said pointedly to her and Maggie, "I love Eddie—he's a dear friend—but we've done him. We've done him to death!" He snatched the *People* from Maggie's assistant and threw it onto Cassandra's desk.

She picked it up and said, "No, no, this is good—this is very good. That psychiatrist is going to trial tomorrow, and the ratings will be through the roof. What's Eddie working on?"

"He's staking out a Jamaican serial killer," Maggie informed.

Hawkins was suddenly interested. "A Jamaican serial killer?" he asked.

Cassandra watched his eyes light up like a kid on Christmas morning and warned, "I don't want blood and guts. I want to broaden the format."

"Listen, Cassandra," Hawkins responded. "I know they brought you in here to raise our standards—to be the journalism cop—"

"Excuse me?" Cassandra asked with some heat.

"—*but I will not let you do this to my show!*" Hawkins said.

"I am *not* the cop here," Cassandra snapped.

Maggie tried to diffuse the situation, saying, "Don't forget—Eddie's always good TV."

"Not when he's drunk," Cassandra said.

"Eddie's got a new cure for that," Hawkins said to the senior producer, whose tits were bigger than her brain.

Cassandra Adams looked at him quizzically. A cure?

Eddie Flemming was taking his cure—sticking his face into a sink full of ice and water in the men's room. Nothing sobered him up faster or better. He felt like Paul Newman in *The Sting.* Flemming was a man of forty-seven, though he looked younger; he was considered handsome by the one group who mattered the most—his public. Women found him extremely sexy; men wanted to be Eddie Flemming. He was a star in his own right: a New York City cop who'd been the subject of an HBO movie. There was talk of a TV series based on his exploits with the NYPD. He had a personal manager, a film and television agent, even a literary agent. He was constantly being photographed at some of the trendier hangouts in downtown SoHo and Tribeca, usually in the company of movie stars and fashion models.

He was in the men's room of a Midtown steak house called Herman's. Eddie was a regular there. Lunch today consisted of a cheeseburger and four vodka martinis. Eddie, in the grand old Irish tradition, liked his booze.

Life was good. He put his hand in his jacket pocket and made sure the little velvet box was still there. It was.

The departing passengers split into two lines as they approached Customs—one for Americans, the other for visitors to the United States. At the end of the visitors' line stood Emil Slovak, a Czech citizen. Slovak was in his mid-thirties, of medium build, with a few days' growth on his face and piercing blue eyes. He squirmed in his old, ill-fitting suit. The flight had lasted twelve hours, and he was tired and unshaven. His eyes told a slightly different story, though. They were smoky, alert, cunning, and aware of people and the activity that swirled around him.

Behind Emil Slovak stood a giant of a man, also a Czech. Oleg Razgul stood almost six feet tall. He was wide like a wrestler, what one would call a real Slavic bear.

Oleg was trying to take pictures with the disposable camera of some newly imported Russian hookers who'd been on the flight with them—despite the fact that they had spurned Oleg's advances throughout the plane ride. Emil slapped Oleg's hand down. "Don't fool around," he said, clearly annoyed.

"Okay," Oleg replied, and promptly held the camera out at arm's length to take a picture of himself.

"Did you hear what I said?" Emil asked testily.

"I want to document my trip to America," Oleg explained.

The Immigration officer was a black man in his mid-forties. His name tag read Rodney Carlton. He was a ten-year veteran of INS who waved on Emil

Slovak with a slightly bored indifference. "Next, please. Next!"

Emil gave his friend one last glare and stepped up to the immigration desk. "How you doin'? Can I see your documents?" Rodney Carlton said.

"Fine," Emil said. "Yes. Sure." He placed his passport down. Rodney Carlton examined it, measuring the rumpled, shifty-eyed Czech standing before him.

"What is the purpose of your visit to the United States today?"

In heavily accented English, Emil replied, "Two weeks' holiday."

"Do you have a return-trip ticket?" Carlton asked now.

"Sure, yeah," Emil said.

"Can I see it?" Looking past Emil now, Rodney Carlton snapped at Oleg, who was about to take a picture of Emil and the Immigration man. "Excuse me—there's no photography in the FIS area!"

Oleg put the camera away, grinning sheepishly.

"Is he traveling with you? Are you two together?" Carlton asked Edgar.

Emil said innocently, "Yes."

Carlton stared at Oleg, "Sir, why don't you come up and join us?"

"Is there a problem?" Emil asked, suddenly feeling panicked.

"No, there's no problem," Carlton said, "but if you guys are traveling together, I want to talk to you together."

Oleg stepped up to the desk. Carlton said, "Can I see your documents? Passport please?" He took Oleg's passport and inspecting it closely asked him, "Are you related?"

"No," Oleg answered. "He is my friend."

Rodney Carlton ran Oleg's passport through the computer imaging swipe. He turned to Emil and said, "Okay—you're a Czech national." He then turned to Oleg: "And you're a Russian national. How do you know one another?"

Oleg opened his mouth to answer, but Emil cut him off, not waiting for his friend to wreck this delicate situation. "We know each other from Prague."

"How long are you planning to stay?"

"Two weeks," Emil answered.

Carlton turned a weary eye on Emil and said, "I'd like him to answer for himself."

"Yeah, but he doesn't speak English," Emil said.

"I speak very good English," Oleg responded proudly. Emil wanted to kill him then and there.

"Then, answer my questions," Carlton firmly said. "Where were you planning to stay?"

"Hotel," Oleg answered. "Cheap hotel."

"What are you planning to do?" Carlton asked.

Oleg replied enthusiastically, "I am here for movies."

"For movies?" Carlton asked, clearly puzzled by the Czech's answer. "Are you here to see movies . . . or *be* in the movies? I don't understand."

"Actually, both, sir. When I was a boy," Oleg explained, "at school I see movie called *It's Wonderful Life*. Directed by Frank Capra. Ever since, I want to come to America. Land of the free. Home of the brave. A country where anyone can be anything."

Oleg paused. "As long as they are white."

Emil interjected, "He was just making joke. Bad joke."

The people in line behind them were getting restless. Rodney Carlton ignored them. He said to Emil, with some heat, "I'm not talkin' to you." The foreign duo was starting to tick him off. He asked Oleg, "How much money are you bringing in?"

"Nothing," Oleg said. "Our friend has money."

Emil stiffened.

"What do you mean your friend has money?" Carlton wanted to know.

"We don't need your welfare," Oleg said, staring

back at the black man. "Don't need stamps for food. Our friend owes us!"

Emil, off to the side, was quietly going crazy. Rodney Carlton continued measuring Oleg, then asked the tall man, "You're here for two weeks. Why would you be thinkin' about welfare and food stamps?"

The line kept getting longer behind them. The other passengers, by this time, were growing increasingly impatient. A senior Immigration officer by the name of Winkler walked over to the desk. He said to Carlton, "What's the problem? What's going on?"

Motioning to Oleg and Emil, Carlton said, "These two are giving me strange responses. I think they should go to secondary."

Winkler surveyed the long line of passengers eager to get through the Customs maze; the natives were getting restless. "Look at the damn line," he said to Carlton. "What time do you want to get outta here? It's lunchtime."

"There is no problem," Emil tried to explain. "My friend is little drunk. First time in airplane." He smacked Oleg in the face, though not as hard as he would have liked to. "Don't waste officers' time," Emil chided him. "They have work."

"All right," Winkler said. "If their passports are in order, let 'em go to Customs."

Rodney Carlton reluctantly stamped their passports. There was something about these guys he didn't like, but there were too many people waiting impatiently behind them that needed to be moved along. It was going to be a long afternoon, Carlton sighed to himself. Better to let his colleagues deal with those two.

Two secondary Immigration officers were grilling Oleg and Emil in an interrogation room. These guys just didn't sit right with either of the officers, much like a six-course Hungarian dinner.

The first officer said to Oleg, "Okay. You work in a vodka factory. I understand that." He turned to Emil and asked, "What kind of work do you do?"

"I am butcher," Emil responded.

The second Immigration man tried to get cute, asking Emil, "You're a butcher? What do you use pig intestines for?"

Emil said, "You stuff sausage with it."

The second officer asked now, "And what do you do with the bones?"

"Dog food," Emil said, and looked over at Oleg. It was his fault they were in this room now: Oleg and his stupid responses to the colored man's questions.

The first officer asked Emil, "Are you married?"

Emil grinned. He asked, "No. Are you proposing?"

Eddie dried himself off with a towel and checked his bloodshot eyes in the mirror. He reached into his jacket pocket and pulled out the small blue Tiffany's ring box. He opened it for inspection. Inside was an engagement ring that had set him back nearly two grand. The woman he planned to give it to was well worth it.

Eddie held the open box to the mirror. He said to the mirror, "Will you marry me?"

That didn't sound quite right, so he tried again. "Wanna get married?"

Still no good. Women liked the slow buildup. Eddie said, trying a different approach, "What are you doin' Saturday?"

Better. Eddie was interrupted by another guy stepping into the men's room. It was Eddie's partner of twelve years, a barrel-chested black man named Leon Jackson.

Eddie said to Leon, "I'm gonna propose to her."

"When?" Leon asked.

"Tomorrow," Eddie said. "Lunch."

Eddie snapped the box shut and put it back into his pocket. He lifted his head and dropped some Visine into his eyes.

Leon asked, "You ready?"

He was, and answered, "Ah, the thrill of the hunt. I love it."

Leon laughed as they walked out of the bathroom. It was time for business, and they were graciously allowing Robert Hawkins to see them in action firsthand. Robert Hawkins was somebody to treat nicely, as far as Eddie was concerned. Hawkins was big TV, and Eddie was liking his celebrity status. True, Hawkins was a bit of a schmuck, but he got the ratings.

TWO

Seeing Times Square for the first time is an overwhelming experience for anyone. Sights and sounds and smells out and out assault the senses. From the thousands of flashing neon signs to the blaring of car horns, to the throngs of people to the towering high-rise buildings, Times Square *is* critical mass. The six-block area has often been called the center of the universe, and there is no place on planet earth quite like it.

To say that Oleg Razgul and Emil Slovak were experiencing culture shock would be putting it mildly. The nonstop action, the bright, blinking lights, four-story-high billboards featuring beautiful women clad in skimpy underwear—all of it left them feeling overwhelmed.

Emil and Oleg lugged their battered suitcases up Broadway, trying to take in everything. They had taken the airport bus into Manhattan, which had deposited them at the Port Authority terminal. Next to New York City, Prague was a blip on the map. At the corner of Broadway and Forty-fourth Street, Oleg took a picture of the Criterion ten-plex movie theater.

"Times Square. Just like in the movies," Oleg said in Russian.

Replying in Czech, Emil said, "Don't speak Russian."

"Why?" Oleg asked in Russian. "Why do I always have to speak to you in Czech?"

Emil snapped back in Czech, "Because I don't like your ugly language. I heard enough of it in school. Now, speak Czech or English. And don't fool around anymore. You almost got us thrown out of America!"

From his pocket Emil pulled out an envelope, where an East Side address was written. He hailed a cab.

Emil glared at Oleg, who smiled sheepishly and turned his attention to the window of a large electronics store on Broadway, the kind with inflated, marked-up prices that preyed on unsuspecting tourists.

Oleg was staring at himself on a video monitor inside the display window, the image fed by a camera that pointed toward the street. Oleg read the sign posted next to the video camera, in almost a reverent tone: "Three-chip color. Color viewfinder. Image stabilization. Solarization. Night vision. Make your own movies."

"We have no money. Come on."

Oleg stared at the camera, wanting it worse than he'd wanted anything in his life. A taxi pulled up. The cabby popped the trunk as Emil climbed inside. He looked out the window—there was no sign of Oleg.

The cabby asked, "Where you want to go, buddy?"

Emil pointed to the return address on the envelope and passed it through the change slot to the cabbie. He said, "Here."

A moment later he saw Oleg hurrying out of the electronics store with a suspicious bulge inside his coat. Moving like an Olympic sprinter, Oleg picked up both suitcases and flung them into the trunk. He slammed it shut and jumped into the backseat next to Emil.

Oleg opened his coat and proudly showed Emil the video camera he'd just stolen. Emil saw a couple of irate clerks charging out of the store in the direction of the taxi.

Emil screamed at the driver, "Go! Go!"

The driver mashed the accelerator, and the cab began to hustle down Broadway. Oleg beamed proudly. America was indeed the land of plenty— if a man was willing to take it.

Eddie Flemming hooked a left turn off Third Avenue and sped east on 144th Street and pulled up in front of a tenement building that, like the neighborhood itself, had seen better days. Vacant lots strewn with garbage flanked either side of the tenement. He stepped out of the car, with Leon Jackson and Robert Hawkins following.

Hawkins asked, "So what's Unique?"

Eddie said, "Not what, who." He handed Hawkins some gruesome Polaroids of a woman on a bathroom floor, covered in thick blood. "He's from Antigua. His girlfriend was taking too long putting her makeup on. They were late for a party. Stabbed her with a beer bottle."

"Jesus Christ," Hawkins said. "That's unique."

"Yeah," Eddie agreed. "And he still went to the party."

Eddie took back the photos and pocketed them. A few yards away, Leon was talking to one of his snitches, a young black man who went by the name of Little Fuzzy. Leon handed Little Fuzzy a twenty and said to Eddie, "Top floor. Back room."

"Yeah," Eddie said. "I make big cases, they make the news, and I look good. But the problem with becoming a star is Downtown—they shoot at stars. Now, be quiet." He put a finger to his lips and added, "Shhhh."

As they approached the entrance to the building, Eddie noticed smoke wafting out of a doorway and spotted empty crack vials scattered on the ground. They almost stumbled over two crackheads when they reached the doorway. Eddie waved them off silently. The crackheads ran off.

"I hope this prick doesn't run. My knees are killin' me," Eddie said. "Stay behind me," he again warned Hawkins, who was eagerly hovering over Eddie's shoulder.

"Are you worried about my safety?" Hawkins asked. "I'm touched."

They reached the back of the tenement, and sure enough, a young, good-looking black man—Unique, no doubt—was simultaneously trying to climb down the fire escape and pull his pants on. Eddie flattened against the side of the tenement, and made Hawkins do the same.

"Just keep your people out of my way," Eddie said to Hawkins.

Hawkins said into his cellular, "You ready?" To Eddie he asked, "Are you ready?"

"Yeah, yeah, Jesus," Eddie said irritably.

Eddie moved in, gun drawn. He heard Hawkins barking at his camera crew over the cellular, "Come on! Come on, you fucking guys. Let's move it!"

Unique was climbing down the ladder that dropped to the ground, but before he could get to the bottom, Leon burst through the door behind him and kicked at the retractable ladder. Unique went flying to the ground, dropping his gun, which went clattering down the alleyway. Eddie and Leon were on him like beans on rice. Leon retrieved the gun, while Eddie yanked Unique to his feet, saying, "What's your rush? Going to a party?"

"Why you chasin' me, man?" Unique wanted to know.

"I don't know—you always come outta your house that way?" Eddie asked, getting the handcuffs out.

"It's not my house, man," Unique claimed, trying to talk his way out of it, knowing already he was doomed to failure. He plunged ahead anyway, adding, "I don't live here."

"Well, then, that sounds like burglary to me," Eddie said, slapping the cuffs on him.

At that moment an unmarked van came careening around the corner and onto the scene. The camera crew, two bearded, twenty-something guys, hopped out and started filming, unaware they'd missed the bust. Robert Hawkins was not pleased.

"Any chance we can do that again?" he asked Eddie.

"Do it again?" Eddie asked. "I didn't wanna do it in the first place."

Later that same afternoon, a cab pulled up in front of an old five-story brownstone on East Eighty-fourth Street between Second and Third Avenues. Emil paid the driver with what little American money they had remaining between them, and then stepped out of the cab. The trunk popped open, but the cabby made no effort to help with the luggage. New York City cabbies were notorious for not helping with luggage; besides, the two foreigners had given him even less incentive to do so—Emil had only tipped him a quarter.

As Oleg retrieved their suitcases, Emil made his way to the half-dozen steps leading to the brownstone's front door. He turned around to make sure Oleg was behind him—the lumbering fool was impossible sometimes. Instead of following, Oleg was on the sidewalk, videotaping him.

Watching the LCD screen, Oleg watched as Emil said sharply, "Turn that off! Get the bags."

"Why should I carry your bag?" Oleg replied.

Emil growled, "For five years I paid for your stu-
pidness—you'll carry my bag for the rest of my life
if I say so." He gave Oleg the steely, challenging
gaze that never failed to send a chill down Oleg's
long spine. "Unless you refuse."

Though he likely could have snapped his smaller
partner into two pieces, Oleg feared Emil. He
tucked the camera into his coat, picked up both
bags, and followed Emil inside. The inside door,
not surprisingly, was locked. In the vestibule, Emil
scanned the names on the intercom until he found
the one he wanted, checking it against the return
address on an envelope he had taken out of his
pocket.

"There," Emil said. "Five RW."

Oleg went to press the buzzer for 5RW, but Emil
slapped his hand away. Instead, Emil pressed all
the other buzzers. Sure enough, some trusting soul
buzzed them in without asking who was there, a
strict violation of Manhattan survival techniques.

They climbed the stairs, Oleg still filming Emil
as they ascended. On the fourth-floor landing, Emil
spotted a crack pipe on the floor. He picked it up
and sniffed it.

Oleg looked at the crack pipe and asked, "What
is?"

"Smells like chemicals," Emil guessed correctly. "For smoking drugs."

Emil pocketed the pipe. They reached the top floor and walked down the dark, dirty, cavernous hallway toward a door at the end.

Inside the apartment, it was dinnertime. Tamina, a pretty Russian lady of thirty-five or so, brought in a plate of hamburgers and fries for her husband, Milos, who was about five years older than his wife. Milos was dressed in dirty plumber's overalls. The apartment was cheaply furnished and decorated, with cheap, gaudy American pop culture crap— Elvis commemorative plates, souvenirs from Disney World and Miami Beach. The only item that stood out was a huge Sony Triniton home entertainment center.

Tamina set the plate down on the table for her husband. She said, "And this is for dessert." She teasingly slipped off her panties from under her dress and placed them on Milos's lap.

Emil was about to knock on the door, but Oleg stopped him. Holding the video camera, he instructed his friend, "Get into position."

"What?" Emil asked.

Oleg motioned with his new toy and said, "First scene of my new movie. Collecting our share from the bank job." He peered into the video camera and cried, "And action!"

Emil played along, hamming it up for the camera as he knocked on the door.

They heard a man say, "Just a moment, please! Just a moment!"

Inside the apartment, they heard footsteps approach. Then Tamina opened the door just a crack—in customary New York style, she left the chain lock securely in place. Peering through the opening, she saw Emil smiling at her. Her blood ran cold. Despite this, she knew she had to unlock the door. Emil pushed his way inside, followed by Oleg, who was filming away.

"Emil?" Milos exclaimed, clearly surprised and more than a little nervous.

"Surprise, surprise," Emil said cheerfully, though Milos looked anything but happy to see them. He shot a horrified look to his wife. Emil danced merrily into the middle of the living room and threw his arms around Milos, giving him a big bear hug and kissing him on both cheeks. He couldn't help but notice the huge gold Rolex on Milos's wrist.

Tamina was wearing a faded housedress—drab along with the furnishings—but it was clear to see that she was wearing an expensive gold necklace, a gold bracelet, and big pearl earrings.

Emil said to Milos in Russian, "Your sister said she didn't know where you were—but you shouldn't write to her with a return address if you're hiding." He waved the envelope to prove his point.

"Did you hurt her?" Milos asked.

Emil smiled, and the effect was anything but warming—his grin was malicious, chilling. "You know me . . . I never hurt anybody," he said.

"Hello, Tamina," Oleg said. He looked her over and liked what he saw—all the right curves and valleys, with an ass he wanted to sink his teeth into.

Milos, frightened but trying damned hard not to show it, barked at the big man, "Take your eyes off her, Oleg!" To Emil he said, "It was not my fault you two were caught." He looked at Oleg with disgust. "It is really his fault! Trying to get the bank clerk's phone number! How could I wait?"

"Yeah?" Emil responded, clearly not caring about the man's frank explanation.

Milos looked panic-stricken. Emil, from the corner of his eye, saw something that displeased him. It was Oleg. The big clunk had Tamina cornered and was videotaping every inch of her body.

Milos barked, "Oleg! Leave her alone!"

Neither Emil nor Oleg knew that Milos and his wife weren't home alone. Through the crack of the bathroom door, a young woman looked out. She had just stepped out of the shower, and her hair was sopping wet. She had a towel wrapped around her slender frame. From the tone of the conversation in the living room, the pretty girl instinctively knew to be frightened.

Emil was saying to Milos, "Let's forget all this shit! Calm down! You know what? Give me my money!"

Milos, still frightened, said to Emil, "We spent it!"

Emil laughed hysterically, but there was little mirth in it. "Give me my money!" he demanded.

"It's no joke—we spent it. Emil, look at the way we live," Milos pleaded. "I'm a plumber. You think I would be working if I had money?"

Oleg grabbed Milos's wrist, showing Emil the Rolex.

"What's going on?" Emil asked angrily. "Just give me my money!"

"Emil," Milos implored. "I will help you."

"You'll help me?" Emil asked skeptically.

"Yes, I get you a job."

"A job?" Emil asked contemptuously.

"Yes," Milos said. "Money is good."

"A job as a plumber?" Emil asked, not believing what Milos was telling him.

"Yes, is easy to learn," Milos said, sensing that the situation was getting out of hand.

Emil was getting angry. "You think I came to America to work? No way!"

Milos said, "We started over—you can, too." Emil's expression was growing more furious. "Emil, please! I am your friend, you know? I'm your friend. Please!"

Emil, irate now, slammed Milos into the refrigerator. He spotted the butcher block near the sink and pulled out a very sharp kitchen knife. In a flash he grabbed Tamina roughly and held the blade up to her throat. Tamina whimpered.

"Emil!" Milos cried. "Put down the knife!"

Holding the knife even closer to Tamina's neck, Emil angrily shouted, "You spent all the money while I was in prison, and now you tell me to get a job as a plumber fixing toilets!"

Emil pulled the knife away from Tamina's neck, then in a blind rage plunged it deeply into Milos's chest. Milos pitched forward to the floor as Emil rammed the knife into him again, then a third time, in rabid fury. Oleg, through the video camera's lens, saw Milos's blood splatter Tamina's face. Oleg, awed, watched openmouthed, but continued filming.

Tamina shrieked in horror and tried to flee. Emil

grabbed her arm, not noticing her gold bracelet fall to the floor. He covered her mouth, holding her tight. Tamina squirmed like an eel, but Emil was too strong for her to escape his grasp. Enraged, in a killing frenzy, he stabbed the knife into her torso repeatedly, her blood spurting all over the worn furniture. Oleg made sure to catch his friend's violent blood lust on videotape. Tamina slumped to the floor, dead. Her eyes were still open in horror.

By the time Emil and Oleg heard the bathroom door fly open and saw a figure dart into the bedroom, it was too late. The bedroom door slammed shut as Emil cursed silently for not checking all the rooms in the apartment. There was a witness—and Emil hated witnesses.

Emil scrambled to his feet and kicked open the warped wooden bedroom door. He saw the open window that led to the fire escape. Together, he and Oleg dashed to the open window and looked out. A couple of flights below they saw a woman making her way quickly down the rusted metal stairs. She was wearing a flimsy summer dress and was barefoot, her red hair still wet. She looked up at them, terrified.

"What a beauty!" Oleg said in Czech.

Emil had to agree. Even though her face was gripped by fear, hers was a timeless, vulnerable beauty; in fact, she was doubtless the most stunning woman either of them had ever seen. They watched as she reached the bottom rung of the fire escape ladder, dropped to the ground, and started tearing down the alley toward the street.

"She saw!" Emil said angrily. He pushed Oleg aside and went into the bathroom. The floor was wet; the girl had doubtless just gotten out of the shower when he and Oleg had stopped by uninvited. Her underwear and purse were draped over a chair. Emil grabbed the purse and started rummaging through it. He found a Czech passport. Inside was her picture. He stared at it for a moment.

"Daphne Handlova," he read, then flipped the page. There was one U.S. Customs stamp in the passport for June 16, 1998, the day she had arrived in America. Underneath the stamped date were the words: SIX-MONTH VISA. "Still here two years later. They'll deport her if she goes to police."

Emil pocketed Daphne's passport and her wallet. He scooped up her shoes and her jacket, walked into the kitchen, then dumped them on the floor. He sat down next to Milos's dead body, trying to think. Inspired suddenly, he jumped up and started tearing through the kitchen cabinets, flinging cans and bottles and dishes aside.

"What are you looking for?" Oleg asked, confused.

Under the sink Emil found exactly what he needed—a can of nail polish remover. He looked down at the bodies and said, "I'm going to make a Bohemian barbecue."

He drew back the kitchen curtains, plunging the room into darkness.

THREE

Jordan Warsaw—he preferred to be called Jordy—jogged through Central Park in a jacket and tie, not far from the boathouse near West Seventy-fifth Street. It was already dark, and most New Yorkers would have questioned the sanity of such an action. The dangers of Central Park after dark were one of New York's most famous urban legends, right up there with alligators in the sewers and subway rats bigger than Lassie. Still, it was the quickest way from the West Side to the East Side of Manhattan when one was in a hurry. Taxis were expensive, and the crosstown bus was unreliable. His 1988 Chevy redcap, fire department issue, had unfortunately crapped out in the middle of Central Park, the victim of a cracked radiator. His beeper had gone off, and having no other choice, Jordy started running across the West Side.

Jordy Warsaw was in his late twenties. He had brown hair and dark, soulful eyes. He was athletically handsome, and often found himself making eye contact, with the promise of much more, with the prettiest women New York had to offer. Since his divorce, though, he'd been a little sour on the opposite sex.

Jordy was dressed for work: a blue suit from Moe Ginsburg's, tie, and slightly scuffed black loafers. He was not a slave to fashion—working for the NYFD, he couldn't afford to be.

He ran up a hill that paralleled the path he'd been jogging on. The slight detour would shave a couple of minutes off his trip and bring him closer to the park exit on East Seventy-ninth Street. As he rounded a corner, one of Central Park's nocturnal denizens leaped out from behind a large elm tree. He was black, young, and menacing, a Harlem homeboy with a bad attitude.

The mugger said, "Yo, man, got any spare change? How 'bout a spare twenty?"

Sounding impatient, Jordy said, "Look, pal. I don't have time for you. Get out of my way."

He tried to push past the mugger, who was a good two inches taller and at least fifteen pounds heavier.

"All right—how 'bout *all* your fuckin' money?" the mugger said roughly.

The homeboy pulled a knife. Jordy had been expecting this. The mugger was quick, very quick, but not quite fast enough. In a whirl of deadly movement, Jordy grabbed the mugger's wrist and disarmed him with a series of martial arts moves. The knife went flying into the night as Jordy hurled the homeboy down to the ground, twisting the mugger's arm behind his back. With his other hand, he pulled a Browning 9 mm from his shoulder holster and jammed the barrel against the back of the homey's head, then displayed his NYFD shield.

"Okay, you're under arrest," Jordy told him. "Now you happy?"

He efficiently handcuffed the mugger, who mouthed a string of obscenities. The homey, feeling like the situation was quickly slipping out of his control, said, "Okay, okay, all right. What are you, the cops?"

"Fire department," Jordy said.

"Man, firemen don't carry no damn guns," the mugger protested.

"Oh, yeah?" Jordy asked. "Guess again."

Now he had an inept mugger to deal with, on top of everything else. He searched the homeboy's coat pockets, pulling out a handful of driver's licenses and credit cards.

"Nice," Jordy said. "How many people you rip off tonight? Get up."

His beeper went off again, and he heard fire engines in the distance. He had to do something with this guy; bringing him along was out of the question. Jordy had an idea that might just work.

The mugger, who liked to describe himself as the Terror of Central Park, struggled to get free, whimpering, "Hey, yo, man. C'mon!"

Jordy dragged the mugger over to a tree. He unlocked the cuffs and told the homeboy to hug the towering elm tree. He cuffed him again so that the mugger's face was pressed up against the bark.

"What you gonna do, man?" the mugger asked, scared now, and with good reason. He'd been subjected to some pretty nasty shit while handcuffed by some of New York City's finest. "Where you goin'?"

Jordy checked his pager. He said to the black dude, "I'm goin' to a fire."

"Oh, hell, no!" the mugger squealed. This wasn't going the way it was supposed to, not at all. He watched as Jordy left him handcuffed to the tree and started jogging off across the park toward the East Side, calling out, "I'll send a cop back for you."

The homeboy cried indignantly, "Hell, mutha-fuckin' no! You can't leave me handcuffed to no goddamn tree! Some freak'll come in here and stab me, man!"

As he made his way over to the other end of Central Park, Jordy heard the mugger cry out, "What you gonna do next—shove a plunger up my ass?"

Nothing draws a crowd in New York City like a fire.

The entire top floor of the apartment house that was once home to the late Milos and his equally late wife Tamina was a smoking ruin. The neighboring buildings and the few trees on the block were black with soot and ash. The other tenants of the building huddled in blankets, waiting to be allowed back into what was left of the building. Fire trucks from three engine companies, red lights flashing, were parked in front of the building. Dozens of radios crackled. Fire hoses zigzagged the sidewalks like overfed pythons. The excited crowd was aching to see some carnage, or at least some heavy flame action.

After changing into a turnout coat and high boots, Jordy pushed his way through the throng of people and made his way over toward the battalion chief, Louis Garcia. He was barking out orders, saying, "Lieutenant, take your line and relieve Ladder Company Sixty on the top floor."

"Hey, Louie, " Jordy said. "Were you first due?"

"Yeah," Garcia said. "I radioed you guys right away 'cause you got two roasts on the top floor. But you don't hafta investigate 'cause Homicide just went up there."

"Homicide?" Jordy asked with some annoyance. "Who said they could go up there? I didn't make this a crime scene yet."

"Hey, it's Eddie Flemming," Garcia replied.

"Yo, Jordy," called a voice behind him. Jordy turned to see Bobby Korfin coming toward him. Korfin was a veteran arson investigator, an overweight, good-natured Brooklyn boy. He was pulling on a turnout coat with FIRE MARSHAL stenciled on the back, and was wearing high rubber boots and a red helmet. Jordy liked him.

"Where you been, man?" Bobby asked. "We got a celebrity."

"So I heard," Jordy said. "Who the hell let him up there?"

"I dunno," Korfin said. "You think Eddie'll give me his autograph?" Bobby Korfin was actually starstruck by the high-profile detective.

Jordy asked, "You see anything in the crowd? Anybody suspicious?"

"Nah," Korfin said. "I'm sure the suspect's not here."

"Oh, yeah?" Jordy asked. "Why?"

" 'Cause Eddie woulda locked him up by now," Korfin replied.

Jordy and Bobby Korfin carefully climbed the charred stairs, greeting the firemen they worked with every day. Jordy had a bad feeling about this one—nothing conclusive, just a premonition that this fire was anything but routine.

Inside the apartment, the smell of smoke and burned flesh was overpowering. The roof was nothing but smoking wooden beams. The clear night sky was actually visible. The apartment floor was a watery, murky swamp.

Eddie Flemming and Leon Jackson were present, Eddie standing on an overturned television set to keep his shoes clean and dry. He gripped a half-smoked Cuban cigar. Leon held a handkerchief over his face. The two bodies of Milos and Tamina were charred beyond any recognition. One thing was clear, however: Something kinky had been going down in this apartment; their bodies were in a very unusual position.

Leon turned to Eddie as firemen dragged hoses

out of the apartment. "So it looks to me, from the sixty-nine position here, that they were doin' each other but were so whacked out of their heads, they set the pipe on the mattress, lit it up, and they got fried. What do you think, Eddie?"

Jordy walked into the apartment, followed closely by Bobby Korfin.

Eddie spotted them and said to Leon, "I don't know, but we got experts here. Why don't you show 'em what you found?" Eyeing Jordy, he said, "I hope you don't mind, guys—we thought maybe you needed some help."

Korfin ignored the slight, making a beeline for Eddie. "Not at all. Detective Flemming, how you doin' today? Bob Korfin. My Uncle Tony worked with you back at the Two-One when you were—"

Cutting him off, Jordy said to Eddie, "Detective, you mind putting out the cigar? We have to pick up scents."

"Oh, sorry," Eddie said, and gently stubbed the cigar out. He carefully slid it into a cigar holder and put it in his jacket pocket to finish later. Cuban cigars, even half-smoked ones, were harder than ever to come by.

Leon Jackson displayed the pipe he'd found at the scene and said, "I found this crack pipe. Looks like they got careless."

Jordy rolled his eyes and said, "I'm glad you guys got it all figured out, but you don't mind if we go through the routine? Gives us something to do."

Eddie shook his head and replied, "No, we don't mind."

Leon chimed in, "No, no. Go ahead."

"Appreciate it," Jordy said, throwing a look at Korfin, who shrugged. As a rule, NYPD Homicide detectives had little respect for fire marshals' investigative skills, regarding the marshals mostly as glorified firemen with badges. Likewise, arson investigators like Jordy Warsaw had little faith in a cop's ability to crack a fire-related crime.

Eddie went through the watery muck in the apartment, moving into the kitchen and living room, checking the apartment out.

Korfin said, "Okay, we got a fast-burnin' fire, got some good patterns—about thirty minutes old."

Jordy moved over to Tamina's body and pulled on a rubber glove. He gently opened her mouth and felt around inside.

"Mouth's clean," he commented.

"Clean?" Korfin asked. This was getting more and more interesting. In the living room, Eddie saw something shiny in an inch of dirty water on the floor. He bent over to take a closer look, and saw that it was Tamina's gold bracelet.

"So let me get this straight," Jordy said to Leon. "You guys think that a couple of crackheads burned themselves up?"

"That's what it looks like to me," Leon said.

"And while they're burning up," Jordy went on, "they're still going down on one another? Gotta hand it to them."

"Yeah, well, some people got their priorities straight," Leon said. His judgment was rarely questioned, and he didn't like this hotshot kid telling him his business.

"Guess they do," Jordy said, and went back to examining the bodies. Jordy noticed a tiny bit of unburned cloth behind Tamina's head. He took a set of tweezers out of his pocket. On cue, Korfin produced a Baggie. Jordy dropped the bit of cloth into the plastic bag.

"Flammable," Jordy explained to Leon.

"What was that?" Leon asked.

"Evidence of a homicide," Jordy replied.

His comment got Eddie's attention immediately, and he walked back into the bedroom.

"A homicide. You fellas know what that is, right?" Jordy asked.

"No, what is it?" Eddie asked sarcastically.

"Bobby, why don't you explain it to them?" Jordy

said to Korfin, then turned to one of the firemen, Ernie Camello. "Ernie, punch a hole in the floor?"

"No problem," Camello said, and pushed Eddie and Leon aside. "Excuse me, gentlemen. You might want to step over just a little more. Don't want to get your pants wet."

Leon and Eddie moved to higher ground, on a half-melted TV set. Eddie handed the gold bracelet to Leon. Camello hacked at the wooden floor with an ax, opening a huge gash. When he was done, the four inches of water on the floor began to drain through the hole into the apartment below, taking all kinds of stuff with it—pictures, housewares, and other items. Jordy went back to examining the body.

Korfin said to Eddie and Leon, "They have no soot in their mouths, which means they weren't breathin' before the fire, and that usually means they were deceased. This little piece of cloth my partner found means they were doused in a flammable liquid and then positioned like this on the bed. To the untrained eye, it looks like an accident."

Jordy, in the meantime, was kicking around on the floor, searching for something in particular. In less than two minutes, he found it.

"What's he looking for?" Leon asked.

It was Eddie who answered: "A timer."

Jordy found some wires attached to an outlet and pulled them out. On the other end was a simple kitchen timer. Jordy handed it to Eddie.

"Here you go," Jordy said. "A big double homicide."

Eddie nodded and said, "Good." For the first time he looked at Jordy, impressed.

"Let's go, Bobby," Jordy said, and together they left, walking back down to the street, crossing over to Bobby Korfin's redcap. "Did you see the look on Eddie's face when you handed him the timer? Damn, I wish I had a picture of it," Bobby said.

"He knew all along," Jordy said.

"What?" Korfin asked.

"Why'd you think he was so quiet?" Jordy asked. "He was testing us."

FOUR

Down on the street, the first of the news vans was pulling up. Before the van even came to a halt, a news crew jumped out the back and went about their business. The party was officially in full swing now.

Eddie and Leon exited the building, Eddie carrying a Baggie with the timer in it. An attractive dark-haired reporter pushed her way through the crowd and stuck her microphone in Eddie's face. He knew her—Nicolette Karas. She was smart, aggressive, and respected in her line of work. She was also very pretty.

She asked Eddie, "Detective, does it look like a murder?"

"We don't know that yet," Eddie responded. "It's much too early. There's a lot to be done."

"How many victims are up there?" she asked.

"There are two bodies found at this point."

"Can we go up to the crime scene?" she asked.

Eddie tried not to grin when he answered, "You know you can't do that. C'mon!"

Undeterred, Nicolette asked, "Is it drug related?"

Eddie, weary of the rapid-fire questioning, said, "We don't know. When I have more I'll let you know."

She motioned for her cameraman to zoom in on the Baggie in Eddie's hand. She continued, "Detective, what's that you're holding in your hand? Evidence?"

Other reporters were arriving by this time, all barraging Eddie with questions. Nicolette was forgotten as Eddie answered their queries easily.

Daphne Handlova, still barefoot and clad in the thin summer dress, her hair uncombed but dry by now, stood behind one of the barricades. A barefoot woman, especially one as beautiful as Daphne, would normally have stood out in any crowd. With all the excitement, however, her presence was barely noticed by the throngs of rubbernecking New Yorkers.

Daphne tentatively stepped out from behind the barricade to signal Jordy. However, her view of him, and his view of her, was blocked by the news crew. He did manage, though, to catch a quick glimpse of her and started walking toward her. But when the news crew moved on, she had disappeared. Jordy walked back to the redcap.

"What is it?" Korfin asked.

"There was a woman," Jordy said. "I think she wanted to talk to us. She looked scared."

Jordy ignored the pandemonium, still searching the crowd for the stunning redhead he'd gotten a glimpse of. Then, like a thunderbolt, he remembered something.

"Oh, shit!" he cried. "Oh, no!"

Six minutes later, the redcap screeched to a stop in the middle of Central Park. Jordy leaped out, with Korfin following. Jordy stopped dead in his tracks when he got to a certain elm tree.

The mugger was still handcuffed to the tree. The difference now was, he was stripped naked, from his gold chain all the way down to his Reeboks. He saw Jordy and started screaming, his eyeballs rolling in their sockets, anger and humiliation the order of the evening.

"Oh, here you come! Here you come! It's about fucking time!"

"What the hell happened to you?" Jordy wanted to know.

The mugger ranted as Jordy unlocked the cuffs,

saying, "She stripped me, man. A bag lady! Stripped all my clothes off, man—grabbin' me all in my nuts. It was disgusting!"

"You should consider yourself lucky, all right?" Jordy said to him. "Because we're not going to lock you up—you're free to go. So why don't you get the hell out of here?"

"A dog pissed on me, man," the mugger said indignantly. "You done violated my civil rights!"

Bobby Korfin said to the mugger, "We got you for robbery one. Let's go—take a walk."

There were a million stories in the Naked City.

Eighth Avenue between West Forty-second and Forty-seventh Streets is New York City's premiere red-light district. Porn palaces, titty bars, X-rated movie theaters, and sleazy flophouse hotels line the stretch of Midtown Manhattan that the locals call Sin Alley. Drug dealing and prostitution flourish openly along the crowded street corners.

It was in one of these sleazy, cheap hotels, on the corner of Eighth Avenue and West Forty-fourth Street, that Emil Slovak and Oleg Razgul had decided to hole up during their stay in the Big Apple. In room 28, the bed was lumpy, the plaster cracked, and the place hadn't seen a new coat of paint since La Guardia had been the mayor.

The crappy TV was tuned into *The Roseanne Show*. On-screen, a middle-aged man was weeping into the camera. Roseanne asked him, "So you slept with your son's wife. What was that all about?"

"I take full responsibility for sleepin' with my daughter-in-law. I had low self-esteem. I thought I had to compete with him."

Emil reached for a paperback dictionary they'd purchased earlier that day. Flipping the pages, he muttered to himself, "Self-esteem . . . self-esteem . . ."

On the TV, the man went on. "Losin' my job, and everything, caused my behavioral disorder." He turned to a younger guy who looked just like him. The older man begged, "Forgive me, Kirk. Let me hug you." The audience booed heartily. Roseanne attempted to mediate.

Oleg sat in a cheap chair, staring into the video camera's LCD screen, rewinding Emil's bloody rampage through Milos's apartment, watching the events in reverse. It was almost comical, the sight of the blood pouring back into Tamina's belly and her body rising up off the floor even though she was dead. Oleg watched, fascinated, a bottle of cheap whiskey between his legs.

Emil sat on the lumpy bed, going through Daphne' Handlova's wallet. He was wearing Milos's Rolex. Tamina's gold necklace and pearl earrings were on the bed in front of him. He pulled some photos out of the wallet. There was one with Daphne posing with a younger girl, probably her sister, on a street in Prague. Another photo appeared to be more recent: Daphne on ice skates at the rink in Rockefeller Center. She was smiling at the camera, and no mistake about it, she was absolutely gorgeous.

Emil looked up. Oleg, the idiot, was videotaping him again. Emil snapped, "Turn that fucking thing off."

"I'm not filming," Oleg explained. "I am watching Milos die. It's just like a movie, but better."

Emil, exasperated, grabbed the video camera from him.

"Don't break it, don't break it, please," Oleg begged in Czech.

"Speak English!" Emil barked.

In English Oleg said, "You said speak Czech."

"How do you erase it?" Emil wanted to know.

"I'll do it," Oleg said. "Don't hurt my camera."

Emil tossed the camera back to his colleague. Oleg caught it and clutched it as if it was solid gold.

"Stupid Milos," Emil growled, and briefly relished the memory of slaughtering Milos and Tamina like hogs. "I didn't want to kill him." He pulled a black card from Daphne's wallet, with a phone number and the words WORLDLY ESCORTS embossed in bright pink letters.

"Worldly Escorts?" Emil asked.

There was a phone in the room, but it needed four quarters for it to work. Emil dialed the number on the card. After two rings, a woman's voice, sounding very sexy, answered and purred, "Hello. Are you looking for companionship?"

The woman on the other end was loud enough for Oleg to hear. He asked Emil, "Whore?"

Emil nodded at Oleg and said into the phone, "I am homesick. You have Eastern European girl? A Czech girl?"

The woman on the other end said, "As a matter of fact, I do have a lovely Czech girl."

"I take her," Emil ordered into the phone. "Send her."

Later that night, Bobby Korfin pulled the redcap up to Fire Station 91, on East Eighty-ninth Street and York Avenue, a stone's throw from the East River. The old Nine-One had been extinguishing fires in the Yorkville neighborhood since the 1920s, when elevated subways rumbled down Second and Third Avenues. In those days, entire city blocks tended to burst into flames, usually in the winter, with the flick of an Ohio blue-tipped match. The firemen of that era had it easy, compared to dousing flames in a seventy-five-story Lexington Avenue high-rise. Tonight's fire had been relatively easy, but still had its dangers. Those old brownstones were tinderboxes.

Jordy and Bobby Korfin walked into the fire station, Jordy saying, "Now that you know him, maybe you can get extra work in the next movie they make about him."

Korfin liked the idea, asking, "Yeah?"

"Maybe you can be his stand-in," Jordy said.

Inside the fire station, the men were pulling off their heavy equipment, coming down from the high of fighting a fire. Jordy and Korfin walked toward the TV room, where the set was playing in the background. On the screen, Nicolette Karas was interviewing Eddie, who held up the Baggie.

Behind them a voice boomed out from the doorway, "What the hell is that? You gave Eddie Flemming the evidence?"

Deputy Chief Fire Marshal Declan Duffy, the head of the arson squad, stomped angrily into the kitchen. Duffy was a gruff, ball-breaking Irishman. It was no secret that he was politicking aggressively for the fire commissioner's job. Neither Jordy nor Bobby Korfin could have cared less personally, but

Duffy, in his quest for higher office, made their lives miserable.

Duffy asked angrily, pointing to the TV, "Who did cause and origin?"

"Who do you think, Captain?" Jordy asked.

"Then, why didn't *you* talk to the reporter?" Duffy asked.

Jordy responded, "Because we got more important things to do, like finding out who did it."

Duffy said, exasperated, "Don't you guys understand? It's all about image. The better we look, the more money I get to pay you guys overtime."

"Yeah, right," Korfin muttered.

Duffy heard everything. "What was that, Korfin?" he asked.

"I said, 'Yeah, you're right, Chief,'" Korfin replied. "As soon as we get something, we'll let you alert the media."

"You do that, wise guy," Duffy snapped. "Now, let's solve this thing before Eddie Flemming does."

Together Jordy, Korfin, and Duffy climbed the stairs to the top, where a door opened into the arson squad room. There were half a dozen cluttered desks, divided into two rows of three each, which cleared a path to Duffy's office. The walls were decorated with yellowing posters of pyromaniacs, arsonists, and even some Middle Eastern terrorists.

Perez, a young, energetic investigator who hailed from the Bronx, looked up from his desk. He said excitedly, "Hey, guys, I got your torch. He just gave a full confession."

A tall, scruffy, unshaven white dude was sitting on a wooden chair beside Garcia's desk. His shabby appearance relegated him to Class-A New York City lowlife and weirdo—the kind that seasoned Manhattanites instinctively gave a wide berth, on the sidewalks or on the subway. The primary difference between this guy and the rest of the mentally disturbed rabble was that this man had a freshly scratched symbol of the cross etched into his forehead. It was quite an eye-opener.

It was Max, the neighborhood arsonist. He specialized in trash can fires and was obsessed with all things combustible. The denizens of the Nine-One knew him well.

Max piped up, "It's my fire! Screw Homicide. I'll tell *you guys* everything." Duffy went on to his office, ignoring Max completely, while Korfin went to pour some coffee.

Jordy, en route to his desk, asked, "What's that on your forehead, Max? That's a nice attention getter."

"Yeah, I'm religious," Max said. "I'm not an atheist like you! Now, are you guys gonna arrest me or not?"

"How did you start the fire this time?" Jordy asked him, sinking into a chair.

"I used an accelerant," Max said proudly.

"Yeah? What kind?" Jordy asked.

Max said to Jordy, "By the way, I'm really sorry about your wife leaving you."

"Max!" Korfin warned.

Max went on, almost gleefully. "Yeah, and with your old man dying last year you—what's it? Just you and the dog now?"

"Max!" Korfin said sharply.

"Does it feel bad?" Max said. "I mean, the new guy your ex-wife's seeing—I hear he's a big shot Downtown."

Jordy had had enough. He jumped up and grabbed Max by the collar. "All right, asshole, you're outta here," he said.

He pulled Max by the collar down the aisle toward the door.

Max said, "That's it! I'm suing."

"Get in line," Korfin said, taking over. He threw Max out of the room. Behind them, Garcia was laughing like hell.

Jordy said indignantly, "What's so funny? How

does he know so much about me? Who tells him my life story?"

"He hangs around downstairs," Garcia said. "The guys talk to him. He's a joke."

"He's no joke," Jordy said. "One day he's gonna graduate from trash can fires and do something serious."

"Okay, okay," Garcia said. "We'll ban him from the station."

Serious journalists, like those who toiled for *The New York Times* or *Sixty Minutes*, regarded *Top Story* as one more cheap tabloid show that spewed its trashy sensationalism into the living rooms of uneducated Americans. They had equal contempt for the show's host, Robert Hawkins, who could have cared less. His ratings were through the roof, the highest in the country for tabloid TV, according to the latest Arbitron reports. His recognition factor ranked up there with Leonardo DiCaprio and the President of the United States.

Inside their crummy hotel room on Eighth Avenue, Emil and Oleg heard the catchy jingle of *Top Story*, then watched as the logo was splashed onto the TV screen. Emil sat on the edge of the bed while Oleg was still in the chair, filming the television with his new toy.

Robert Hawkins appeared on-screen, intoning seriously, "Tonight, *Top Story* brings you an exclusive interview with Stephen Geller, who horrified the nation two years ago when he went berserk and murdered three clerks in a Manhattan shoe store. But now, Mr. Geller's claim, spoken softly and articulately, is that *he* is the victim. According to Mr. Geller, the events of that fateful day were not his fault, but rather the fault of his psychiatrist. Hard to believe . . . watch."

Oleg panned the video camera over to Emil, who looked at Oleg and said, "Louder."

Oleg, still peering through the viewfinder, saw his own hand reach out and turn up the volume on the TV, where the scene was jump-cutting to a shot of a mental hospital interview with Stephen Geller, conducted by Robert Hawkins. Geller was surprisingly preppie-looking, maybe twenty-one or twenty-two years old and well groomed and polite, the antithesis of the mad-dog murderer the media made him out to be.

Geller said, "This had nothing to do with shoes that didn't fit or my relationship with my father, who, as you know, made a fortune selling penny loafers in the fifties. These people died because of the criminal actions of my doctor."

"Your doctor?" Hawkins asked.

"Yes," Geller said. "My psychiatrist didn't insist that I stay on my medication."

The two foreigners watched as Robert Hawkins leaned forward in his chair. He asked Geller, with a touch of sarcasm in his voice, "So you feel absolutely no responsibility for killing these people?"

Geller responded, "It was my finger that pulled the trigger—but I'm not morally responsible. My psychiatrist knew what I was capable of. How could I know? I'm not a doctor."

"You're pretty savvy for a man who's been found mentally incompetent to stand trial," Robert Hawkins said.

Stephen Geller looked insulted. He replied, "Look, I'm a victim here, too. I was a year away from getting my master's in art. Now I'll never graduate. My life has been permanently disrupted."

"Permanently disrupted?" Hawkins asked him. "Aren't you selling paintings now for quite a lot of money? Hasn't this 'incident,' as you call it, jump-started your career as an artist?"

"Look," Geller responded. "I'm in here. You call this a career move?"

"And isn't there a movie in the works about you?"

"We're in negotiations—that's correct," Geller said.

Hawkins asked now, "Doesn't the Son of Sam Law prevent convicted criminals from profiting from their crimes?"

Emil leaned forward, straining to hear the TV over the noise from the streets and other hotel rooms. He was riveted.

Stephen Geller said, "That doesn't apply to me because I'm not a criminal. *I'm not a criminal! I wasn't convicted.*"

Emil said to Oleg, "I love America. No one is responsible for what they do."

Three sharp knocks sounded on the door. Oleg swung the camera over to it, filming, then swung it back to Emil, who said to him, "Get in the bathroom."

"Whatever we do—we fuck her first, right?" Oleg wanted to know.

Emil ordered, "Oleg, get in the bathroom and shut up!"

Oleg did as he was told, but left the bathroom door open just enough to peer out with the lens of his video camera. Emil shut off the television. Tamina's kitchen knife was sticking out of his boot. Emil pulled the cuff of his pants over it, then opened the door. His face immediately registered disappointment.

The girl was not Daphne. She was a tall, leggy blonde.

She called herself Honey, but her real name was Wanda Schlanger from Greenpoint, a predominantly Polish neighborhood that sat neatly on the Queens/Brooklyn border. She was twenty-six years old, but already a veteran of the New York hustling game. Her mother, who had come from a small village in her native Poland, died when Wanda was fifteen. Wanda's face wasn't much to look at, and she was a bit on the skinny side, but fortunately, she'd been amply endowed with a fine pair of breasts. Six months later, her father, who was drunk more often than not, took his pleasure from his young daughter whenever he wanted. There was no one in the small, shabby apartment to stop him. When Wanda was sixteen, she smashed a vodka bottle over her father's head and took all the money in his wallet—sixty dollars. She took the subway to Manhattan and found a place to live in the basement of a Polish church on East Ninth Street in the East Village. In exchange for a place to crash, Wanda cooked, cleaned, and had sex with Father Kowalski, who knew some tricks her drunken father had never dreamed of. A year later, Wanda moved into a SoHo loft with a bunch of third-rate musicians and traded sexual favors for a bed, sometimes taking on the drummer, the bass player, and the lead guitarist all in one night. She drank, did lots of drugs, and generally partied all the time. From there it was a short hop into the world of prostitution. With her good looks and bodacious bosom, she worked steadily for one escort service after another.

"Hi," she said seductively. "I'm Honey." She didn't see Oleg videotaping her from the bathroom.

"Where is Czech girl?" Emil demanded.

"Baby, I'm anybody you want me to be," Honey said. "I'm a little schoolgirl. I'm Mommy. I'm a Czech girl."

Honey walked into the room, closing the door behind her, and started undressing. Seasoned professional that she was, she said to Emil, "I like to get business out of the way before we get down to pleasure. Why don'tcha put my money on the dresser?"

Emil said sternly, "I ordered Czech girl. Daphne— you know her?"

From the bathroom, Oleg zoomed in on a close-up of Honey, who said, "It's an out-call service run out of an apartment. I don't meet the other girls."

As the little scene unfolded, Oleg whip-panned, zoomed in for close-ups, and attempted every trick a video camera was capable of.

Emil asked the whore, "Where is escort service?"

"That's confidential," Honey said. "Could you put the money on the dresser?"

"I like to talk to the person who runs the service," Emil said. "Can you give me address?"

Honey was getting impatient. Time was money. She said to Emil, "Look, do we have a problem here? There's no reason to have a problem. I'm gonna make you feel real good. You want a Czech girl? After I'm done with you, you won't miss her. Now, why don't you pay me?"

She started unbuckling Emil's belt, hoping that would get the ball rolling. Instead, Emil stopped her and said, "Listen to me. I don't want sex. Just give me the address and then you go."

Honey's countenance turned hard as nails. "Look, man, I don't give a shit if you want sex or not, but you're payin' for my time."

Emil furiously yanked the knife out of his boot and shoved Honey up against the door. He pushed the blade against her throat, his blood getting very hot. The image of slaughtering Milos and Tamina was still fresh in his mind.

"Give me address!" he shouted.

"All right, all right," Honey cried. It was turning into one of those days. "Don't hurt me, please! It's in my book, in my purse."

Emil backed off. Honey reached for her bag. Had Emil Slovak been more experienced with this sort of business transaction, he would have grabbed the purse himself. As it was, he barely had time to notice the can of mace—the prostitute's best friend—Honey whipped out of her bag. She gave Emil a healthy blast in the face, more than was necessary.

Emil stumbled backward as Honey frantically snatched up her clothes. She made a beeline for the door and managed to unlock it and open it six inches, but Emil, even half blind, was too quick. He slammed it shut, rubbing his eyes, blocking the door.

Oleg was catching it all on tape. Through the viewfinder, he saw Honey dart like a rabbit toward the bathroom. She pulled the door open and was greeted by the sight of a second man, this one a giant wielding a video camera. In her panic, she barely noticed that he was laughing at the whole sorry spectacle. Seeing no refuge in the bathroom, Honey stopped on a dime and spun around, ready to make another shot at the door. Before she could move an inch, Emil was there. He smashed her solidly in the face with his fist, a blow so hard she was propelled backward into the grimy bathtub. She flailed wildly with her arms and lost her balance, falling helplessly. She grabbed the shower curtain for support, ripping it from the rod much like Janet Leigh in *Psycho*. She landed flat on her back in the tub, the shower curtain falling on top of her.

Emil, his blood lust bubbling, descended on her like a panther out for the kill. He brandished the kitchen knife and slammed it down into Honey's gut, once, twice, three times, spraying crimson all over the bathroom. Oleg watched it all through the viewfinder, lovingly catching it all on tape. Stephen Spielberg, eat your heart out.

Honey's cries for mercy were muffled by the mildewed shower curtain wrapped around her face. Emil brought the knife back up and rammed it back into her belly again.

Women. They just couldn't be trusted.

FIVE

It was almost Daphne.

Jordy stared at the face on the rendering and said to the composite sketch artist, a middle-aged woman named Sue Malone, "Her lips are fuller than that. You can see 'em a mile away." Sue Malone smirked; Jordy sounded almost dreamy.

They were in the arson squad room at Fire Station Nine-One. The squad room was empty except for Jordy, Korfin, Garcia, and Malone, who had about fifty unfinished sketches piled at her feet. It was close to dawn, and all of them were exhausted. Half-empty Chinese food containers and coffee cups were scattered all over the place. Korfin watched the sketch artist do her stuff while he talked on the phone.

"How about her cheekbones?" Sue asked.

"Her cheekbones are prominent and her eyes

were huge," Jordy said. "Big blue eyes—and when I saw her, she looked scared. Like she was looking to get away. But she was absolutely beautiful."

Sue Malone gave Jordy a look. Again, he sounded dreamy describing her. Jordy noticed this and said, a little defensively, "I got a good look at her."

Korfin was speaking with the landlord of the burned-out brownstone where the bodies had been found. "From Czechoslovakia?" he asked. "How long they been living in your building?"

He jotted down "4 years" on a notepad.

"All right," Korfin said into the phone. "I'll be in touch when we know somethin'." He hung up and said to Jordy, "Milos and Tamina Karlova. They were quiet, kept to themselves. Landlord don't know who the girl is."

"How long they been livin' here?" Jordy asked.

Korfin turned to Garcia. "You hear the question, Garcia?"

"Yeah," he said, cradling the phone between ear and shoulder. "I got Immigration here. They've been here illegally."

"Well, they're definitely permanent residents now," Korfin said, adding, "I got the owner of the plumbing company Milos worked for."

Korfin said, "Why don't we get some sleep, and we'll go see him in the morning?"

"You can go on home," Jordy said. "I'm taking your car and going back to the crime scene."

"Aren't you tired?" Korfin asked.

"If I go home, I won't be able to sleep anyway," Jordy said.

He looked at the sketch of Daphne that the artist had printed out—it wasn't a bad likeness. He headed for the door; Korfin fell in behind him. As they passed Garcia, he handed them the address.

Korfin looked at the sketch. The girl on it was a knockout and no mistake.

Korfin said, "She the one keepin' you up? Like to meet her, huh? She'd make you forget your ex-wife. Cure your insomnia."

Jordy gave his partner a dirty look, grabbed his coat, and disappeared into the night.

Jordy pulled up in front of the East Side brownstone in Korfin's redcap. The sun was just beginning to poke up behind the East River and Roosevelt Island. Yellow crime-scene tape zigzagged the sidewalk in front of the building. A young uniformed cop stood watch, stifling a yawn. Jordy flashed his badge. The uniform became alert.

"Yeah, go ahead," the uniform said, then yawned again.

Jordy took the stairs three at a time. He entered

what was left of Milos and Tamina Karlova's apartment. The first rays of the morning sun poked through what had yesterday been the roof of the building. The stench of burned brownstone was overpowering, but Jordy's experienced sense of smell also detected the aroma of fresh cigar smoke.

He walked into the back room, which faced the courtyard behind the building. He struggled to peer through the darkness, looking through the muck and char of the room. Jordy heard a voice in the darkness ask, "Mind if I smoke?"

Eddie Flemming was sitting on a barbecued armchair. On the arm of the chair was a brown legal folder and stacks of photographs from the crime scene. In his other hand, Eddie was holding the photographs of Milos and Tamina's charred corpses.

"It's your crime scene now," Jordy answered. "You can do whatever you want."

"Did you catch the news?" Eddie asked.

"Nah, I must've missed it," Jordy said.

"Well, just so you know," Eddie said, "I gave you guys all the credit."

Jordy considered it, then said, "Well, just so you know, I don't care about that stuff."

"Nah, why should you?"

"I don't even watch TV."

"Good," Eddie said. "That's commendable." He poured some vodka from a bottle next to him into an empty wonton soup container, and added some orange juice. He knocked it back.

"Did you get a report from the M.E.?" Jordy asked.

Eddie said in return, "Let me ask you something . . . you got a problem with me?"

"Look," Jordy said. "If you showed up and found me stepping on your crime scene—and remember, it was my crime scene yesterday—it might piss you off, too." He paused, then added, "So, what about the report?"

Eddie said, "Yeah. They were both dead before the fire. You were right. They were killed by a knife. Eight to ten inches long. Maybe a kitchen knife. The male was stabbed so hard the killer broke off the tip of the knife in his spine. And that usually indicates something pretty personal."

Jordy brought out the sketch of Daphne and handed it to Eddie, saying, "The superintendent said he'd seen her before, but she didn't live here."

Eddie admired the sketch. "Prettiest suspect I've had in a while."

"Suspect?" Jordy asked. "What makes you say suspect?"

"What would you call her?" Eddie asked pointedly.

"Look," Jordy said. "I'm not sure she has anything to do with this." He tried to take the sketch back, but Eddie wasn't ready to relinquish it just yet. Jordy continued. "I saw her outside after the fire—I thought it was a lead. Maybe she saw something. That's all." He couldn't get the red-haired beauty out of his mind, and he hated it.

Eddie picked up the crime-scene photos and went over to the burned mattress where the bodies had been found. Not looking at Jordy, he said, "Obviously they weren't having sex. As you pointed out. Why would the killers take the trouble to position the bodies like that?"

"Maybe it's a ritual thing or someone trying to send somebody a message," Jordy said. "Burial rites are taken very seriously in Eastern Europe. It could even be to humiliate them. Just burning them up, no proper funeral—it's just like condemning them to hell."

"Eastern Europe? Like what? Romania? Hungary?" Eddie asked, impressed.

"Or the Czech Republic," Jordy said. "The Slavs have been fighting the Germans and the Russians for a thousand years. These are very intense people, and they take things personally."

Eddie's cellular went off. He clicked it on, listened, then asked, "Yeah? Where? You sure it was a knife? Uh-huh . . . really? Okay."

This got Jordy's attention. It perked him up, despite the fact that he'd been wavering from lack of sleep. He couldn't remember the last time his head had hit a pillow.

Eddie killed the connection and stood, tucking the cellular away. He said to Jordy, "We've got another murder—in a hotel on Eighth Avenue. A stabbing. Clerk said a Russian rented the room."

Eddie moved quickly, still holding the sketch of Daphne.

Jordy said, "I'll come with you."

Eddie couldn't help but smile a little. He said, "This isn't a fire. There'll be nothin' for you to do."

Jordy, starting to like the guy, sarcastically said, "I'll watch you, Eddie. Maybe I can learn something."

"This isn't homicide school," Eddie said.

"My parents are from Poland," Jordy said. "I can help with the Eastern European angle."

Oleg panned down to the front page of the *New York Post*'s early edition, which had just been delivered in three heavy bundles to the newsstand on the corner of Forty-fourth and Broadway in the very heart of Times Square. The headline blared "DOUBLE HOMICIDE—FLEMMING'S ON IT." Underneath was a photo of Eddie Flemming holding the kitchen timer by the wires—the same kitchen timer that Jordy had discovered. Oleg then panned over to Emil standing in front of the newsstand, reading the headline. Emil had changed into a clean suit—the only one he had left. They hadn't bothered checking out of the hotel after killing Honey. They'd simply packed their few belongings and sauntered out into the night.

The news vendor was cutting the blue plastic cords off the bundles. Oleg turned the camera on himself, and smiled into the lens. He said for posterity, "This is second day in America. First day was very exciting. Full of thrills and chills. Over there is costar of my new movie, Emil."

Oleg turned the camera around, filming Emil as he tapped Eddie's picture on the front page of the *Post.*

"Who is he?" Emil asked the vendor.

The vendor replied, "New York's finest. Yeah, that's his case." He picked up a copy of *People* magazine, which had a photo of Stephen Geller on the cover.

"Magazine and newspaper, this all you want?" the vendor asked Emil.

Emil pointed to the picture of Stephen Geller and asked, "Do you know how much killer gets for movie rights?"

Holding up the copy of *People*, the vendor said, "In here, says he wants a million."

"A million?" Emil asked, astonished. "You're kidding. The killer gets one million dollars for television interview?"

The vendor said, "Well, Ted Bundy—famous serial killer—tabloids paid him half a million for *his* interview. And how much you think Monica got for writing a book about the President coming on to her?" He added thoughtfully, "It pays to be a killer or a whore in this country. You want the magazine or not?"

Emil said to the newsie, "Yes, both."

"And these," Oleg added, picking up copies of *Film Comment, Movieline,* and *Premiere*. He knew he wouldn't be able to understand any of it, but there were lots of pictures in them, and *Movieline* had a cover photo of the sexy American movie star Michelle Pfeiffer. Oleg had seen some of her movies in Prague. She was what the Americans called a "knockout."

Emil paid for the magazines as well, and said to Oleg, "Get taxi."

Oleg tucked the magazines into his coat, picked

up the suitcases, and stepped out into the street to hail a cab. He was getting good at flagging down taxis, which was a useful ability to have in New York. As Emil collected his change from the newsie, he spotted an old blind woman waiting at the cross-walk. The light was blinking its green WALK signal; trouble was, the traffic was bumper to bumper at the intersection where Emil stood. Broadway and Seventh Avenue merged into four-lane pandemonium. The old girl wouldn't get two feet before getting broad-sided by any number of trucks or buses.

Emil hurried over to where she stood and asked, "May I help?"

He gently took her arm and escorted her to the other side of the intersection to safety. "Thank you. You're such a gentleman," the woman said gratefully.

Emil watched her walk away, tapping her cane, into the mass of humanity on the city streets. The sight of the blind woman stirred something inside of him. Twelve hours earlier he was mercilessly slaughtering a whore in a bathtub; now he was helping an old, blind lady cross the street.

Life was funny.

Eddie Flemming walked into the crummy King Edward hotel room, with Jordy in tow. The room was swarming with New York's finest: detectives, the crime-scene photographer, uniforms, and paramedics. A detective named Mike Collins was stripping the bed and putting the bedding into a big clear plastic bag. A crime-scene photographer, a pretty young lady named Kathy Jacobs, was standing in the doorway, snapping off one picture after another.

Leon Jackson had already arrived, and was barking out orders: "Mike, you're going to get all the linen, right? Need to run that to the lab right away. Kathy, get a shot of all this before anyone moves it."

When Eddie and Jordy entered the room, Leon said to Eddie, "Victim's taking a bath." He turned to Jordy and said: "P.D. only. Sorry."

"He's okay," Eddie said to his partner.

Shrugging, Leon went on. "We've still gotta run some prints. This kid here from Midtown caught the case."

A young detective, maybe twenty-five or twenty-six, extended a hand to Eddie. He was all excited—the legendary Eddie Flemming in person.

The young detective said, "Tommy Cullen. Heard a lot about you. This is what we got: Figure her to be a prostitute. Judging from the defense wounds on her arms and hands, she was really fightin' for her life. Right this way—in the bathroom."

"After you," Eddie said.

"Room was registered to a Francis Capra," Cullen said.

"Capra?" Jordy asked. The name had a familiar ring to it, something to do with Christmas. "That's not Czech or Russian. Who said he sounded Russian?"

"The clerk," Cullen replied.

"Check the switchboard," Eddie said to the young detective. "Let's see what calls came from this room."

"I'm on it," Cullen said dutifully. "Excuse me, gentlemen."

He left. The others moved into the bathroom. If Wanda Schlanger, a.k.a. Honey, had been fighting for her life, she'd clearly lost the battle. The bathroom looked like a slaughterhouse Eddie'd once seen in the Bronx. Dried blood was splattered all over the walls, and the floor was covered in sticky crimson pools. She was topless, lying in the tub with the bloodied shower curtain half wrapped around her. Eddie recognized Gil Murphy, the medical examiner, dusting for prints.

Eddie took out his cigar holder, and pulled out what was left of the Cuban. He relit it slowly, taking his sweet time. The body wasn't going anywhere, and besides, his thought processes worked better when his lungs were filled with some sweet Cuban cigar smoke. He glanced down at Honey's ruined body in the bathtub.

Murphy said, "Clothes were off in the other room. Tub is dry except for the blood."

Eddie absorbed that little bit of information, then said, "Any of you guys take a piss lately?" He pointed to the toilet seat, which was up. Murphy and the other cops all shook their heads.

"Dust the seat," Eddie suggested. Murphy grimaced, but went about his work.

Eddie stood in the blood-splattered bathroom, studying the scene. The cigar had already gone out. He scanned the dried blood on the wall.

"Only one guy checked in?" he asked.

"Yeah," Leon said.

Eddie said to Jordy, "C'mere. You wanna go to homicide school? Make yourself useful." He positioned Jordy behind the tub, adjacent to the wall.

Eddie said, "The killer's standing over there slashing her. She's fightin' him. The blood is splattering this way. It's on this wall"—he pointed to the wall to Jordy's right—"and there're some specks over there." He pointed to Jordy's left. "There's nothing here because someone was standing right here. Someone big. And he's got blood on him . . . lots of blood. He walked out of here like that."

Eddie turned to Murphy and asked, "Gil, what kind of knife you think we're talking about here?"

Murphy pulled out a clear plastic ruler and went over to the blood-splattered wall. He made some quick measurements and said, "Well, if you look here where he missed and hit the wall, you see that the marks aren't deep, but they're kinda wide. This isn't your everyday kitchen knife or pocketknife."

"Was the tip broken off?" Eddie asked.

"Could be," Murphy said. "Then we should find it here somewhere."

"I think we already found it," Eddie said.

He and Jordy exchanged a look. It was Jordy's turn to be impressed now. He was beginning to understand the legend that was Eddie Flemming.

Tommy Cullen returned and reported, "There was only one call from this room last night. I dialed it—it's an escort service."

"Did you identify yourself?" Eddie asked him.

"Hey," Cullen said. "I'm new, but I'm not stupid."

"Well, call communications and let's get an address on the number," Eddie said.

Cullen held out a slip of paper with the address

of the escort service already written down. "Good work," Eddie said.

"Thanks," Cullen said gratefully. Wait until he told his friends that Eddie Flemming was impressed with his police work. They'd shit little green apples in envy.

Eddie had seen all he needed to see. Leon would oversee the rest of the crime-scene investigation. Eddie made his way down the stairs of the shabby King Edward Hotel——and wouldn't the old British monarch be spinning in his grave if he ever saw the hotel that had been named after him?

Jordy was right behind Eddie. "So you gonna head over to the escort service?" he asked.

"You got any better ideas?" Eddie replied.

"Mind if I come along with you?" Jordy asked.

"This has nothing to do with your fire," Eddie said brusquely.

"But what if it does? You might need my help."

They walked through the lobby and out onto the street. A crowd had gathered to gawk at the crime scene. It never failed—even the most jaded New Yorkers loved a crime scene.

A man approached them, middle-aged and well dressed. He said, "Hey, Eddie! Can I get an autograph for my son?"

Jordy felt a small pang of jealousy. Maybe being famous wasn't so bad after all.

Eddie signed the autograph for the man, saying to Jordy, "I'll let you know what happens."

"Come on, Eddie," Jordy complained. "This is ridiculous. If I ride along with you, at least we can talk about the case."

Eddie allowed himself a small grin. The kid had balls, if nothing else. "All right, I'll tell you what— I'm gonna bounce this coin. If you win, you come with me. If you don't win, you don't come."

"I'll call it," Jordy said. "Tails."

Eddie skillfully bounced the quarter off the pavement. It bounced up, and in the same beat, Eddie caught it and slapped it onto the back of his hand. A trick, Jordy mused, Eddie Flemming had doubtless picked up on the mean streets of New York.

"Heads, sorry," Eddie announced, and pocketed the coin before Jordy could catch a look at it. Eddie started climbing into his unmarked vehicle.

"C'mon, c'mon," Jordy protested. "That's bull-shit—I didn't see it."

Eddie shrugged and produced the quarter again. He said, "Okay, I'll call it. Heads."

Jordy flipped the quarter this time. It came up heads.

"See?" Eddie said. "Now you lost twice." He

started up the car and said to Jordy, "See you around."

Jordy stood on the sidewalk, looking like a puppy that had just been kicked out onto the street during a blizzard. Eddie was about to pull away from the curb; instead, he called to Jordy, "C'mon."

Jordy's face brightened. "Yeah?"

"Yeah, c'mon," Eddie said.

Jordy went for the passenger side door of the car, but before he could reach for the handle, Eddie abruptly pulled away. A real comedian was Eddie Flemming. Jordy stood dejected until Eddie slammed on the brakes. Jordy went over and said, "Is that supposed to be funny?"

What some people wouldn't do for a laugh. Jordy got in, and Eddie sped off down Forty-fourth Street. Despite the traffic, they made it over to the East Side in minutes, thanks to Eddie weaving in and out of traffic, careening around clusters of pedestrians crossing against red lights, and almost broadsiding a hot dog vendor on East Seventy-second Street.

Eddie pulled the Ford up in front of a very fashionable high-rise condo building on Second Avenue and East Seventy-eighth. The doorman was about to tell them not to park in front of the building, but he instantly recognized the great Eddie Flemming.

He kept his mouth shut as Eddie and Jordy walked into the lobby. Eddie flashed his badge and asked the doorman a question. Satisfied with the answer, he and Jordy boarded the elevator and went up to the twenty-second floor.

As they walked down the narrow hallway to apartment 2207, Jordy said, "Thanks for letting me come along."

"No problem," Eddie responded. He flipped the lucky—or unlucky—quarter to Jordy. "Souvenir." He turned and knocked on the apartment door.

Jordy caught the quarter, not quite understanding what Eddie meant at first—until he realized that Eddie had suckered him with the coin toss. Then he looked at the quarter a little more closely. It was heads on both sides. He was starting to like Eddie more and more.

"Two heads," Jordy quipped.

"Better than one," Eddie said.

Behind the door, a woman's voice asked, "Yeah? Who's there?"

"Police. We just wanna ask you some questions," Eddie said.

The door didn't open. The minute the two cops had gotten into the elevator, the doorman had called up and tipped off his tenant that the law was on their way up. The woman said in a muffled voice, "Do you have a warrant?"

On the other side of the door, Jordy said, "We're not lookin' to bust you, ma'am."

The woman was a hardcase. "Then what do you want?"

Eddie had had enough. In a commanding tone he said the magic words: "It's Detective Eddie Flemming from Homicide. Just open the door. We wanna talk to you."

Without hesitation they heard the unmistakable sounds of tumbling bolts unlocking and chains flicked off their catches. The door opened. A woman stood there. She was in her mid-thirties, sleek, pretty, very well dressed in the finest fashions from Prada and Gucci.

She said gushingly to Eddie, ignoring Jordy completely, "Oh, my God—what an honor! Rose Hearn! Oh, please come in! I just saw you on TV!"

Eddie glanced self-consciously at Jordy, as if to say, *What can I tell you?*

"Thank you," Eddie said.

The apartment was beautifully furnished. She may have been a madam, but Rose Hearn went first-class all the way. For all intents and purposes, she seemed to earn a very nice living.

"Just give me a second," Rose said, and moved over to a phone and finished a conversation in a strange language—Afrikaans, it sounded like to

Eddie. Rose Hearn spoke excitedly, and her guests understood only two words: *Eddie* and *Flemming*.

They looked around the apartment. In the dining room, two young girls were working the phones, taking orders for Rose's clientele. Two other girls were working the phone sex lines. Business appeared to be brisk, even at that early hour.

She hung up and turned to her guests. If Eddie Flemming was paying her a visit, some serious shit was swirling in New York City. "What's wrong?" she asked him.

"We don't have her I.D. yet, but I think we found one of your girls murdered last night at the King Edward Hotel," Eddie said.

"Oh, my God," Rose cried. "Honey! Honey's dead?"

Jordy asked, "Do you remember the man who called?"

Rose answered, directing her response at Eddie, "Yeah. He wanted a girl from Czechoslovakia, but I sent Honey 'cause once they get there, you know, it doesn't really matter. Honey was . . . killed? Poor girl . . ."

Eddie sensed her grief, but this was business. He plowed ahead, asking, "Do you have any Czech girls working for you?"

"No," Rose answered.

"Did you tell him you did?" Eddie asked her.

A tall, stunning woman clad only in a sheer leopard robe and skimpy bikini walked into the room. Rose spoke to her in Afrikaans, saying, "Boy, she's so popular all of a sudden."

"What are you saying?" Eddie asked.

"Daphne," Rose said. "Another guy came in asking me about her, too."

Jordy pulled out the sketch and unfolded it. He showed it to Rose, who studied it, racking her brain.

Jordy asked, "This her?"

She said, "Yeah, sort of. I tried to recruit her and gave her my card. I never heard back from her, though."

Rose's friend commented, "Beautiful eyes."

"Who came by looking for her?" Eddie asked.

"He said he was her cousin," Rose said. "I told him where she works. They were just here."

"Describe him," Eddie said.

Rose said, "Tall, short-haired, scary eyes. Second guy with him was . . . shorter, with a wrestler's build. And he wouldn't turn his video camera off me."

"He had a video camera?" Eddie asked, sounding anxious. "Where is she? Quickly!"

"A salon on Sixty-third and Madison," Rose said.

"What's the name?" Eddie asked now.

"Ludwig's," Rose said. "She works there. She washes hair."

Eddie Flemming and Jordy Warsaw got what they'd come for. They didn't stick around for the bagels and cream cheese Rose was about to offer them.

SIX

Eddie drove even more recklessly as they made their way uptown on Third Avenue, running stop-lights and not slowing for anyone foolish enough to get in the way. Which was especially impressive, given that Eddie had vodka and OJ in a soup cup between his legs. This time around, though, he had his siren blaring. Taxis, buses, trucks, bike messen-gers, and skinny Chinese food delivery boys all gave him a wide berth—nothing cleared a Manhat-tan avenue faster than a flashing blue orb and an ear-splitting siren.

They were both on their cell phones, punching in numbers frantically, Eddie doing it with one hand on the wheel, darting in and out of traffic with as-tonishing dexterity.

Eddie barked into his cellular, "Leon—meet us at Sixty-third and Madison—"

Jordy snapped into his, "I'm on my way with Eddie—"

Eddie said, "Hair salon—"

"—Sixty-third and Madison," Jordy said.

"—Ludwig's."

"—The suspects might be there already," Jordy said.

Jordy disconnected. Eddie drank from his wonton soup cup. He said to Jordy, "You thirsty?"

Jordy answered, "I'm on duty."

Eddie replied, "So am I," then took another healthy gulp.

The storefronts and pedestrians along Third Avenue were a blur as Eddie shot up to Madison Avenue, despite the fact that the five-lane street was clogged with vehicles. His drinking did not affect his driving at all.

Eddie said, nostalgically, "I always wanted to be a cop when I was a kid. I dreamed of running up to a door, kicking it in, pulling my gun, and yelling *freeze* at the bad guy. What'd you dream about?"

"Running up to a burning building, kicking down the door, rushing into the smoke and saving a kid," Jordy replied.

"Then, I guess we're doing this the right way, aren't we?" Eddie gripped the wheel as they passed the Madison Pub, one of his favorite watering holes. "If we pull up to a burning building, I'll gladly let you go in first."

Jordy said nothing. Eddie Flemming had a knack for telling the truth.

Ludwig LeRoy liked to tell people he'd been born into a working-class family on the mean streets of Red Hook, Brooklyn. The truth was, his real name was Jeffrey Weintraub, and he was from the fashionable, well-to-do Long Island town of Woodmere. Eleven years earlier, when he was nineteen, he'd told his mother that he was pretty sure he was a homosexual. There was a lot of weeping and hand-wringing. Four years later, when he graduated from Adel phi University in Garden City, Long Island, with a degree in liberal arts, he announced to his family that he wanted to become a hairdresser. There was more weeping and hand-wringing, but this time, with a loan of fifty thousand dollars from his father the podiatrist ("And that's a lot of bunions and in-grown toenails," Dr. Arthur Weintraub declared), he rented a small store on Manhattan's Upper East Side, set up a small salon, and he was in business. He changed his name to something exotic, Ludwig LeRoy, figuring anything sounded sexier than Jeffrey Weintraub. Now, six years later, he was making money hand over fist. He had a dozen hairdressers working for him, and each week he permed, hennaed, and bleached enough hair to stretch all the way to Karachi, Pakistan. He owned a three-bedroom condo in Greenwich Village, a beach house on Fire Island, and a country place two hours north of the city in a town called Rhinebeck.

Oleg had never seen anything like Ludwig's.

He'd started videotaping the moment he stepped through the door. None of the hairdressers or backup personnel gave him much thought, as there was always a news crew or a fashion shoot going on at one time or another.

Oleg said into the sound device, "Hunting begins!"

Through the viewfinder, Oleg saw her—with her flaming red hair, she wasn't hard to spot. Oleg grabbed her arm and spun her around. The girl wasn't Daphne, though she could have passed for Daphne's sister. "I'm looking for Daphne Handlova?"

The girl said, in a Czech accent no less, "Daphne? In the back. Probably shampooing a customer's hair."

Oleg spotted her mixing some hair dye and talking with a funny-looking man, the kind, Oleg saw, who preferred men to women. The man was saying to her, "Why are you messing with your hair color again? You're going to *kill* your hair. You won't look good with black hair."

Daphne responded, "I want to do it. All right?"

Ludwig said, "Well, then do it after work. A customer's waiting."

Daphne prepared to handle the next customer when she spotted Oleg—and the man was filming her. She backed up, trying to get away from him, and made for the emergency exit.

She pushed the heavy metal door open and stepped into the alley. Oleg followed her, still videotaping. Daphne ran as though her feet were on fire. As she rounded the corner, she ran smack into Emil, who was holding a sharp pocketknife.

She squealed in horror. Emil wrapped his hands around her shapely neck. Daphne closed her eyes, turning her pretty little head away, terrified and expecting to be lying dead in moments. For his part, Emil was more than prepared to kill her there and then, but her striking beauty captivated even a hard-hearted Czech such as himself. It caught him off guard.

"I . . . I have a temper," he stammered in Czech.

Oleg continued filming.

Daphne looked at him, uncomprehending.

Emil went on. "When I lose it . . . I lose control.

I didn't intend to kill Milos, but he stole from me. Cheated me! When I went to prison, they beat me, and I still did not tell them he was my partner. I loved Milos like a brother. I'm not a killer!"

There was an uncharacteristic softness in his voice, as though he was trying to rationalize his homicidal behavior to her.

They both heard the back door of the salon open. Emil shoved the knife back into his pocket. Ludwig peered around the alley corner. What he saw was Daphne leaning against the wall and some man holding her closely. Ludwig had nothing against quickies, but preferably not during working hours.

"Daphne darling, will you be coming back to work?" Ludwig said to her.

"In a minute, Ludwig," she called back, grateful that he might very well have saved her life.

Ludwig threw her a knowing smirk, thinking Emil was more than a casual friend if they were doing it in the alley like a couple of mongrels in heat. Well, he thought, why not? She was a lovely girl, and would be an ace hairdresser someday if her hormones didn't keep getting in the way. Ludwig disappeared from view, stepping back into the salon.

"Smart girl," Emil said to her. "I'm glad you're not a whore."

Oleg, as usual, was horning in on his partner's action with the video camera. Once again, Emil snapped at him, "Stay back!"

He reached into his pocket. Daphne stiffened, expecting the knife again. He pulled his hand from his pocket—no knife, she saw with relief—and shoved something into her palm, closing her fingers around it.

He said, "I don't want to kill you. But if you talk, I will." He tapped on her hand and whispered in her ear, "I thought you would like these."

With that, he made himself scarce, disappearing down the alley toward Madison Avenue. Oleg, still taping, kissed Daphne on the cheek. It was like being kissed by a cold, dead herring. Oleg followed Emil down the alleyway.

"Daphne?" Jordy asked just then, appearing out of Ludwig's back entrance.

When she didn't reply, Jordy said, "I'm a fire marshal. You remember me from the other night? You are Daphne, right?"

She still did not respond. Jordy urged, "You don't have to be afraid. We're here to protect you. Come with me. We want to talk to you. And speak English, all right?"

Eddie came into the alley and, as was his habit, took charge of the situation, saying to Jordy, "I got it, I got it. I smell smoke across the street," meaning he wanted Jordy to make himself scarce. This was his ball game now. He took Daphne by the arm and ushered her back inside Ludwig's, saying to her soothingly, "It's okay, it's okay."

Daphne Handlova instinctively distrusted the police, as did most everyone else in her native country. They were brutal, corrupt, and violated virtually every law they were sworn to uphold. She assumed automatically that American police were cut from the same cloth.

Eddie noticed that she was clutching something in her fist. Eddie opened it—and saw Tamina's brushed gold necklace.

"Did he give you this?" Eddie asked. "Was he just here?"

Eddie frantically searched the street, and noticed two suspicious-looking characters on the far corner, standing in front of a fancy dress shop. The bigger of the two was videotaping them. At that moment two cars pulled up, one unmarked, the other a redcap. In the first were Leon Jackson and Tommy Cullen; Bobby Korfin hopped out of the redcap.

As Leon exited the salon, Eddie said to him in a hushed tone, "Across the street—two guys with a video camera." Leon started to look; Eddie said, "No, don't look, don't look! Let's just box them in."

Leon said to Tommy Cullen, "Stay with the girl."

The four of them—Eddie, Leon, Jordy, and Bobby Korfin—strolled casually across Madison Avenue, doing their damnedest not to attract the attention of the two shadowy figures. Their efforts failed, though. Emil took off up Madison Avenue while Oleg stayed behind and continued filming the approaching lawmen.

Emil shouted at him, "Put the fucking camera down! Let's go!"

When he got it into his thick skull that the policemen were coming for him, he, too, booked, charging up Madison right behind his partner.

Eddie and the others started running in hot pursuit. As they darted into the intersection of Madison and Sixty-third, Emil and Oleg's path was suddenly blocked by a double-decker tour bus filled with tourists. Oleg neatly ran around it and seemed to vanish into the crowds that had stopped to watch the chase. Jordy jumped onto the tour bus and scanned the passengers, looking for Oleg. Dead end. Eddie, in the lead, was quickly running out of breath.

"Split up!" Eddie cried, and he and Jordy went off after Oleg, not exactly sure where he'd gone. Leon and Bobby Korfin took off after Emil, who had turned west on East Sixty-third, toward Fifth

Avenue and Central Park. Leon saw him run into a fancy café, the kind with tables and fine stemware lining the outside of the building. Perfect. The little bastard had cornered himself.

Gun drawn, Leon approached the café. He took a few steps toward the entrance. Emil darted out— Leon would say later he never even saw him coming—and whacked Leon on the side of the head with his fist, a surprisingly forceful blow for such a little man. Leon fell backward and crashed into a table occupied by three Park Avenue matrons. Leon's gun dropped to the floor. Emil vaguely realized that Oleg had suddenly materialized and was filming the action.

Emil scooped up Leon's gun and got down to business, pistol-whipping the helpless detective and beating him to a pulp. Frightened diners got up and fled, screaming from the grisly scene. Savvy New Yorkers knew better than to get involved in any way, and that included coming to Leon's rescue.

Satisfied with his handiwork—Leon's face now looked like a pulped pizza—Emil took Leon's wallet, holding onto the gun.

Oleg, the clunkhead, was actually laughing. "Emil, look!"

Bobby Korfin was running toward them, pushing through the fleeing crowd. Oleg swiveled and caught Korfin in his sights, still rolling the video-tape while Emil aimed and fired twice at Bobby Korfin. He was blown backward, bouncing off of a Toyota Tercel parked illegally, and then crumpling to the ground.

"Perfect!" Oleg said gleefully, a regular Cecil B. Demented. "Cut! Print!"

Rounding East Sixty-third, Eddie and Jordy heard the shots and tore toward the café. Emil and Oleg took off down the street, making straight for Central Park.

Eddie and Jordy went to Bobby, who was shot in the side and leaking large amounts of blood all over the sidewalk.

"I'm okay, I'm okay," Bobby gasped. "They went toward the park!"

Eddie went to help his partner. Leon was conscious, but barely. He was a tough old bastard. "Are you hit?" Eddie asked him.

"He got my piece," Leon said dejectedly.

Eddie was already up, leaning over a parked Lexus, taking aim at Emil, who was running his ass off and was almost a block away. Eddie knew it was an impossible shot—the creep was pretty much out of range, and there was always the chance of hitting some pain-in-the-ass bystander. Nonetheless, he shut one eye, aimed, and squeezed off a shot just as the two were climbing the wall. They hopped down and vanished into the wilds of Central Park. Halfway across the intersection, he saw Emil topple. Just as quickly, he saw Emil scramble to his feet and run.

Jordy looked at Eddie in awe. Eddie Flemming wasn't called the best for nothing.

"Did you get him?" Jordy asked.

"I don't know," Eddie muttered. "I think so."

Eddie holstered his weapon and pulled out a handkerchief. He started dabbing the gashes on Leon's face.

"Motherfucker was filming the whole time!" Leon said, sounding really pissed off despite his wounds.

"I know. Relax," Eddie said, trying to calm his partner. "Take it easy. Don't worry—we'll get those fuckers."

SEVEN

Eddie and Jordy watched as Leon, now on a stretcher, was loaded into an EMS vehicle. Bobby Korfin had been taken away minutes earlier. The injured men would be taken to New York Hospital, one of Manhattan's better hospitals.

"Man, but am I havin' a bad day!" Leon said to Eddie.

"You're gonna be okay," Eddie assured him.

After the EMS truck left, its sirens wailing, Eddie and Jordy turned to go back into the restaurant, which had emptied out completely except for the owner, a man named Phillip Amarand. He was co-operating every step of the way with the cops. True, the patrons had run off without paying, but the publicity his restaurant would receive from the bloody incident was worth millions. Curiosity seekers would be lining up for months to eat in the place where there'd been a big shoot-out. In December of 1985, a Mafia big shot named Paul Castellano, along with his bodyguard, Tommy Billoti, had been ambushed outside a joint called Sparks Steak House on East Forty-fifth Street, gunned down by a crew of killers headed by John Gotti. It was a classic gangland hit, and made front-page headlines from coast to coast. As a result, business at Sparks tripled. A restaurant owner next to Sparks was heard to say, "If I'd known the publicity Sparks was gonna get after the Castellano hit, I'd have dragged their bodies in front of my joint."

Jordy had joined Tommy Cullen in the back of the restaurant. Cullen had brought Daphne, who was seated at a table.

A news van pulled up. The camera crew piled out and started filming, followed by Nicolette Karas. The crowds started gathering, pushing and shoving their way to the front of the mob, hoping to get on TV. Nicolette wasted no time sticking the microphone in Eddie's face.

"Detective," Nicolette asked him, "can you tell us what happened here?"

Eddie gently pushed her away and said, "I can't talk right now. We have some things to take care of."

Nicolette Karas was not easily discouraged. In her

line of work, being persistent was a way of life. A cop tried to block her way, but Nicolette would not be stopped.

"I understand, but I noticed that the fire marshal is here with you," she said to Eddie. "Is this somehow related to the fire department?"

"I really can't give out any information at this point," Eddie said curtly.

"I understand your partner, Leon Jackson, was injured. Is that correct?" Nicolette Karas asked.

Eddie answered, "Yeah. Not seriously. He just took a beating, but he'll be fine."

Nicolette knew from experience that Eddie had said all he was going to say. She said to Spiro, the cameraman, "All right, cut!"

Spiro stopped filming and lowered the camera from his shoulder.

Sounding concerned, Nicolette asked, "You all right, Eddie?" Even a stranger would have sensed that there was more to Eddie and Nicolette Karas than met the eye.

"Yeah. Now's not a good time," he said.

"All right," Nicolette said, a little hurt.

"All right?" Eddie asked again, making sure she knew.

"All right," Nicolette said.

Walking back inside Café Amarand, Eddie found

Jordy talking to Daphne. He was telling her, "Just be willing to cooperate."

Eddie was punk sore. His partner was going to the hospital and the guys that had done it had escaped. He was in no mood for any bullshit. "C'mon, start at the beginning. You know these people?" he pressured Daphne.

Daphne knew he meant business, so she cooperated. "Tamina was a friend of mine. My shower was broken, so she let me use theirs."

"Yeah," Eddie said. "Go on."

Daphne fell silent. Eddie cautioned, "Whether you tell us or not, we'll find out. Better if it comes from you."

"If I tell you, will you arrest me?" Daphne asked.

"Arrest you for what?" Eddie asked. "Why would we arrest you?" Daphne hesitated. Eddie added, "What are you hiding? Why are you afraid?"

Jordy piped up, "She just saw two of her friends killed. They probably threatened her."

"Is that all there is?" Eddie asked. "Are you here illegally? 'Cause you don't have to worry about that. We'll talk to Immigration. They're not gonna deport you."

Daphne stiffened—Eddie had hit the nail squarely on the head. He was momentarily distracted as he watched Nicolette Karas and her crew pack up and leave. He felt a small twinge of guilt at his harsh words to the reporter. Jordy watched Eddie watch Nicolette.

"No, don't talk to Immigration," Daphne said.

"Why not?" Jordy asked, snapping his attention back to the lovely Czech.

"Something back home?" Eddie asked now.

Daphne looked at Jordy for some help, but he remained silent. She looked back at Eddie, who wasn't relenting an inch. She was trapped and she knew it. Her eyes filled with tears.

"My little sister and I shared a flat," she finally said. "I came home one night and a man was raping her. His gun was on the chair. I grabbed it. He came at me and I shot him."

Jordy was in serious danger of falling in love with her. He said, sounding optimistic, "That's a justifiable homicide."

Daphne said, "Yes, I know, but . . . he was a cop."

"A cop?" Eddie asked.

Daphne seemed even more scared now than she'd admitted it. Policemen were policemen, be it in Eastern Europe or in America, and they stuck together.

Her words dripping with bitterness, Daphne said, "I was living in a small town in Slovakia. It's like the South here in America. The police are always right. The civilian is always wrong. I fled."

"Look," Eddie said impatiently, "we can help you, but right now we have to deal with what's happening here. Tell us the truth—is that the truth?"

"You're a cop," Daphne said. "You'll never believe me."

She looked like a sad-eyed puppy that had been kicked one too many times. Jordy wanted to hold her in his arms. "Hey, Eddie, can I talk to you?" he said.

They stepped away from Daphne. Eddie didn't take his eyes off her. She tried to listen in on their conversation. Eddie whispered, "She's fucked. Even if her story is true."

"Raw deal," Jordy said.

Eddie tilted his head slightly, measuring Jordy, seeing what the man was made of.

"Look, would you mind letting me talk to her first?" Jordy asked. "Any leads I get, they're all yours. Just let me have first crack at her."

"You wanna talk to her alone?" Eddie asked, tilting his head and peering at Jordy closely.

"Yeah," Jordy simply said.

"What would your girlfriend think of that?"

"I don't have a girlfriend," Jordy answered.

"My point exactly."

"I'm serious here," Jordy insisted.

"So am I," Eddie replied.

"Look," Jordy said. "You intimidate her, 'cause you're a big hotshot celebrity. Me, I'm a nobody. Maybe she'll open up with me. Maybe she looks at me different." He half sounded like he was trying to convince himself at the same time.

Eddie allowed himself a little smile. "You're gonna be her savior? Is this the girl you're gonna save from the burning building?"

"You know what I'm sayin' here," Jordy said.

Eddie gave it some thought, his expression impassive, gauging Jordy's sincerity. Finally he said, "Okay, I'll give you a head start. But you get her to the station house. Don't let her out of your sight. She's the only warm body we got left."

"C'mon, I'm a professional, all right?" Jordy said.

"I know," Eddie responded, "but women like her have a way of turning professionals into amateurs."

Before Jordy could respond, Eddie turned and disappeared into the mob scene outside.

EIGHT

Emil rolled down the sock on his right foot. What he found was a bloody mess. The cop's bullet had grazed his ankle, but the wound was still deep. The pain was excruciating.

He could hear Oleg draining his bladder in the bathroom stall behind him. They were in the restroom of a seedy little diner on Third and East Eighty-first—a joint so dirty Emil wouldn't have let his dog eat there, if he'd had a dog. The owner looked at them suspiciously when they'd come in—the limping man and the hulking giant with the video camera made quite a pair. One frigid look from Emil was all it took to keep the little man quiet.

Emil pulled off his left sock and shoe, lifted his foot into the small sink, and turned on the faucet. He washed the blood away, which exposed the hole in his ankle—the bullet had blown a fairly substantial chunk of flesh out of it. Emil plugged the wound with toilet paper, then cut the stiff cloth towel from the dispenser with a knife and wrapped it around his bleeding ankle. He gritted his teeth in agony.

The toilet flushed. Oleg stepped out of the stall, zipping up. He saw Emil's wound, and commented, "Ouch! Emil . . ."

Emil hoisted his wounded foot from the sink. Oleg washed his hands, then picked up the video camera and prepared to film, adjusting the fluorescent light above the grimy sink.

"What are you doing?" Emil asked angrily.

"Gotta light the scene better," Oleg explained. "Like, make it more dramatic. Just like a scene from *The Third Man*."

"Shut up," Emil said.

"It hurts, huh?" Oleg asked.

"This is nothing," Emil said, even as the waves of pain washed over him.

Emil grunted. Oleg and his goddamned Kodak moments. Emil pulled his shirt up and exposed his bare back to Oleg, who looked away in disgust.

"Oh, Jesus. I hate looking at that," Oleg said. Emil's back was a sight he did not wish to see more than once in his lifetime.

"Don't you want to film this?" Emil asked grimly.

"No," Oleg said, and finally shut off the camera.

Jordy headed down Second Avenue in Bobby Korfin's redcap. Daphne was in the backseat. Jordy watched her in the rearview mirror. His emotions were at war—she was a suspect in a double homicide, but he wanted her all the same. It did not make for a healthy situation.

Daphne asked, "Now I become custody of police department?"

"If you cooperate with the DA," Jordy said, "maybe they'll help you with your situation."

"I will if they don't send me back," she said.

"They won't until this is over," Jordy said.

She looked away, staring out the window at Second Avenue. She looked back at him, tears in her eyes, and asked, "Are you married?"

He looked at her in the rearview mirror and said, "Divorced."

"Do you live alone?" she asked. When Jordy didn't answer right away, she added, "Because I've been in these clothes since . . . the killings. Maybe we could we stop at your place? I could just . . . take a shower before I go into custody."

Your place. Jordy gripped the steering wheel harder than necessary. Was she trying to manipulate him—beautiful women were masters at that game. Or did she genuinely want to clean up before the inevitable shit hit the fan? It was a tough call, the toughest one he'd ever had to make, and for all the wrong reasons.

Finally he said, "Look—I—I can't take you back to my place."

She nodded like she understood, then turned her attention to looking out the window.

It was do or die time for Eddie Flemming.

He stared into the mirror at P. B. Herman's and said, "I want to talk to you about something serious." He held up the diamond engagement ring. He said, "I want to live the rest of my life with you . . . I do love you, and—"

He noticed a small dab of Leon's blood on his shirt cuff. Nothing like a little blood for proposing to a woman. At that moment Paulie Herman entered, carrying a towel and a vodka tonic.

"She's here," Paulie said.

Paulie set down the drink, and the silent ritual began. He handed Eddie the towel. Eddie wiped his face and hands, then gave the towel back to Paulie. Paulie helped Eddie on with his sports jacket. Eddie took a small bottle of Visine out of the jacket pocket and squeezed a few drops in each eye.

He straightened himself up and looked in the mirror, taking a big gulp of the drink. He set the glass down and started out. Paulie handed him a bottle of Binaca. Eddie sucked down a few drops and left the bathroom, Paulie right behind him.

It was lunchtime, and P. B. Herman's was crowded. Eddie came out of the men's room and sat down at the table—his table. He took the ring box out of his pocket, holding it under the table.

Nicolette Karas walked up to Eddie from behind and have him a kiss on the cheek.

"Hey, honey," she said.

"Hey," Eddie said.

Speaking Greek, she ordered a drink from the waiter, who was also Greek, then sat down across from Eddie at the table. Neither of them spoke, looking at each other instead.

She asked, sounding miffed, "What is your problem? Why did you snap at me? I just wanted a statement."

"I can't answer you just because you want me to answer you," Eddie said.

"Okay," Nicolette replied, "but you didn't have to embarrass me in front of my colleagues. You could give me something."

"Well, I'm sorry," Eddie said. Women . . . "Did I embarrass you, sweetheart?"

"Stop it," Nicolette said.

Eddie looked at her. She was a beauty, with high cheekbones and olive skin. "Maybe I should just, you know, turn to the cameras and say 'Do you mind if we just work something out?' " he continued dryly.

"All right, Eddie," she said. "Don't patronize me."

"I'm not," he said.

"Yes, you are," she responded. "I'm not just some reporter. I don't just stick the microphone in your face. You could give me something."

"Yeah, well, you took the camera and put it right down on the evidence," he said. "That was—"

"That was *good*," she said. "You were holding the evidence."

"You were merciless," Eddie countered. "You didn't give a shit if you got me or not."

"And who was it that taught me how to do that, huh?"

"You're ruthless," he said.

"You're not so bad yourself," she said, and grinned. "C'mere."

They kissed, long and hard and passionately. A moment later Nicolette said, "Look at this—you have blood on your shirt. Whose is it?"

"Could be Leon's," he said.

"Last week you came home with blood on your

shoes," she said. "What am I going to do with you?"

Eddie took her hand and said, "You know what I was thinkin'?" He faltered, searching for the right words. "These shoes might look nice with another pair of shoes next to them in the closet."

Nicolette looked at him incredulously. He went on. "You know, Nicky, I've been married twice before. My first wife was a professional woman, didn't have time for children. And my second wife—I never wanted to go home to her."

Nicolette's eyes brimmed with tears. Was Eddie going to finally utter the words she wanted to hear? Before he could continue, though, her cellular started ringing. Eddie stopped and looked down at it.

"What are you doing?" she asked. "What are you saying?"

The cellular continued ringing annoyingly. Eddie stared down at it.

"Eddie?" she asked. The tiny little phone kept ringing. She said, "Don't worry about the damn phone. I won't answer it."

"Answer the phone," he said.

"No," she said. "Tell me what you want to say."

"Answer it," he said.

"Okay, but hold the thought just for a second,"

she said, clicking the phone on. "They only call me when it's an emergency. Just hold the thought." She said, into the phone, "Can you call me back?"

Eddie heard the voice on the other end say, "We need you here in twenty minutes. Get in a cab."

"What are you talking about?" she asked.

The disembodied voice on the other end said, "Katie—we don't know where she is—we can't find her. You gotta anchor the five o'clock. This is your shot. Come now."

Eddie slid the ring box into his pocket as she hung up, saying, "Okay . . . okay . . . yeah."

She turned to Eddie and said, sounding excited, "They want me to anchor! They want me to anchor tonight!"

"That's good," Eddie said, sounding decidedly unhappy.

Realizing she'd likely ruined a momentous occasion in their lives, Nicolette said, "But I can't go now. We're in the middle of something here."

"No," Eddie said. "Go ahead. You're gonna be great."

"Listen to me," she said. "I want to know what you're talking about. You know—the shoe thing and the marriages and—"

"I'll tell you tonight," Eddie said. "As soon as you get back we'll talk."

"You promise?" she asked.

"I promise," he said. "We'll talk. You'll be great. Just imagine that . . . just look into the lens and imagine you're talking to me."

"Yeah, I'll do that," she said, "as long as you're not patronizing me."

"Patronizing you? Nah," he said. "I love you."

"I love you, Eddie," she said.

They kissed and then kissed again. Their relationship was not well-known by the general public in New York City, who doubtless would have approved. Everybody loved Eddie Flemming.

"Okay, till tonight," she said.

"Tonight," he echoed.

"You promise?"

"Yeah, I promise," he said.

"Okay," she said, getting up excitedly. "Maybe I'll swing by my place, grab a couple pairs of shoes and maybe just test them out next to yours. Would that be a good thing?"

"Yeah, a good thing," he said. "See you later. And good luck. Don't be late."

She left. Eddie was beginning to really hate cell phones.

Jordy Warsaw unlocked the door to the Nine-One, which was pretty much empty, unusual for a fire station. "The men are out—practicing putting out fires," Jordy explained.

"So . . . the station is empty?" Daphne asked.

"Yeah," he said. "C'mon. The showers are up here."

He gestured up the stairs. Up they went, into the locker room. It smelled like dirty socks and sweat and stale smoke. As they walked, Daphne's eyes never left Jordy.

"You considered becoming a prostitute?" he asked her.

"Yes, I considered it," she said.

"Did you ever turn tricks before?" he asked, praying silently that she hadn't.

"No."

"What about back home?" he asked.

Daphne stopped dead and looked at him, wanting to be angry at his line of questioning. But she found she couldn't, not at this man who seemed so desperate to help her. "When I came here, I had no money. You know—I didn't know anyone. I was by myself. I couldn't get a job because you need a green card. They approached me . . . I could have made a lot of money. I considered it but . . . it's not who I am. They pay me below the table at Ludwig's."

Jordy wanted to believe her, wanted it more than

he'd ever wanted anything. "So you've never been a prostitute?"

There was a long pause before she asked, "Why are you asking me?"

"I'm just trying to find out who you are," Jordy replied.

Daphne studied him, looking hard into his eyes. He was a handsome American man. He wanted her, of that she was certain. She had seen that look in the eyes of many men, both in America and back home.

Sensing an opportunity, she asked him, "Can you let me go?"

She leaned in closer to him, giving him every chance to kiss her. He was tempted, she could see, very tempted.

Jordy wanted to scoop her up in his arms and kiss her, kiss her long and passionately. Instead, knowing he would likely not get this chance again, and knowing he had a job to do, he said, "Showers are this way."

She was desperate now, willing to do anything to gain her freedom. Once she was in police custody, and once Emil and Oleg were behind bars, Immigration would deport her. She was an illegal, and they would send her back to Slovakia. She would be executed. The courts would show her no mercy—she had killed a policeman, and that was serious business. Even her sister's testimony would be useless.

"You could shower with me," Daphne said now.

It was an extremely difficult offer to resist, especially when Daphne whispered something in his ear, in Czech. He wasn't certain what she said, exactly, but he got the general idea—something to do with the joys that could lie ahead in exchange for her freedom.

Reluctantly, he broke away and gestured once more toward the showers—giving in would mean his career. It would bring shame down on the department and shatter his life forever. Daphne looked away, devastated. Her one bid for freedom had perished.

She headed for the shower stalls. Jordy followed her, saying, "I'll . . . uh . . . get you a towel."

He left her there alone to fetch a clean towel from the cabinet on the other side of the locker room. Daphne surveyed the place. On the far wall was a window. She quickly made for it.

Jordy reached for a towel, which naturally was on a top shelf. His beeper suddenly went off, and he checked the number. He recognized the ten-digit number but decided to ignore it. He returned to the shower stall, clutching the clean towel. He could hear the shower going full blast. Then he noticed the window, wide open, which opened onto the street. It was a harmless ten-foot drop.

"Shit!" he muttered angrily, and rushed to the window. He looked out onto the quiet street. There was no sight of Daphne anywhere. But there was no way she could have disappeared that quickly. He looked back at the shower—he couldn't see through the thick plastic curtain. He pulled it back.

Daphne was huddled in the corner of the shower stall, holding herself. She was also naked, he couldn't help but notice. She looked up at him, tears streaking from her eyes.

"I'm not a whore," she said, sobbing. "I'm not a whore!"

"I know," he said, and now he believed her. He managed to turn the water off, then squatted down next to her in the stall.

"No, you do not know," she said. "I was desperate—that's not me. I shot a cop. Can you imagine what they'll do to me when I go to prison?"

"Look," Jordy said. "They're not gonna send you right back."

"I'm sorry," she said. "I didn't mean to . . . I'm glad. Actually, I am glad it's over. All this time . . . hiding . . . never being able to look anyone in the eyes . . . always afraid that someone would find out who I was. Never trusting anyone . . ."

He covered her with the towel and pulled her to her feet.

"You can trust me," he said to her.

She threw her arms around him, and this time it was no act. He instinctively knew now that she trusted him. Awkwardly he put his arms around her, trying again to comfort her. He liked the way she felt in his arms. It seemed natural, somehow.

Yeah, he liked holding her. Liked it a lot.

NINE

Oleg videotaped everyone in the restaurant, a Midtown eatery called Hamburger Henry's on West Forty-fourth Street. He'd just finished the prime sirloin, french fries, and a soggy salad, washed down with a pint of Bud, all for the low price of $18.95, a bargain by Manhattan standards.

Oleg turned the camera onto Emil, who was wrestling with a small plastic bottle of Extra-Strength Excedrin. Emil was sweating like a pig, burning with fever. Eddie Flemming's bullet was taking its toll.

Emil managed to get the cap off, then yanked out the big wad of cotton, wincing with pain. He up-ended the bottle to his mouth. A dozen Excedrin tablets tumbled onto his tongue. He chewed them furiously, then washed the whole bitter-tasting mess down with a big sip of beer.

He looked up at Oleg and said, "The video of Milos and Tamina—I told you to erase it."

"I did," Oleg said.

"And the whore's murder? You didn't erase that, either, did you? Don't lie," Emil said. "I won't be angry."

"Why not?" Oleg asked.

"Put the camera down, Oleg."

Emil eyed his partner. Poor, crazy Oleg and his delusions of Hollywood grandeur. The pinhead was probably rehearsing his Academy Award acceptance speech in his tiny little brain this very moment.

Emil ignored him and pulled out a small address book from Leon Jackson's wallet. Emil flipped through the address book, looking up Eddie Flemming's address.

"What is that?" Oleg asked.

"What does it look like? It's an address book," Emil said, sounding testy. He looked terrible, Oleg thought—all pale and sweaty.

"Let me get a shot of it," Oleg said, grabbing the video camera and jumping up.

"Sit down," Emil ordered.

"This way," Oleg instructed, focusing on the address book. "Hold it this way." He got the shot and sat back down. He asked Emil, "Why won't you be angry at me for keeping my movie?"

Emil ignored him. He dropped some cash on the table—most of the thirty dollars Leon had had in the wallet. He got up and limped away. Oleg followed, filming everything along the way.

A throng of reporters was clogging the entrance to the 23rd Precinct as Jordy pulled up. He opened the back door and pulled Daphne out. The press descended on them like vultures, sticking microphones in their faces and firing off a barrage of questions.

Inside, Chief Declan Duffy was pacing back and forth in front of the sergeant's desk. Duffy checked his watch every ten seconds, growing more and more aggravated as every second ticked by. The media was hounding him for a statement on the juicy murder story that was still breaking on what had been a very, very slow news week.

Jordy and Daphne walked in. He was surprised to see his superior standing there. Duffy's face, already ruddy from a fondness for single malt scotch, was now a dark crimson color.

Duffy called out, "Hey, Warsaw!"

"Hey, Chief, what're you doing here?" Jordy asked.

"What am I doing here? I came to see how the investigation was going," Duffy said, and he didn't sound pleased. He looked at Daphne, then added to Jordy, "You know, I called and you're not here. I wait up at the station house, you never show the hell up! I beep you—you don't return my call. Where the hell have you been?"

Jordy stepped away from Daphne and approached Duffy, saying in low tones, "Look, Ladder twenty-one was on the Rock for training, all right? So we stopped there so she could get cleaned up."

"What do you mean, cleaned up?" Duffy wanted to know.

"I let her take a shower," Jordy said.

"A shower?" Duffy asked, not believing his ears. "And did you take one, too?"

Jordy felt his dander rising. He said, "No! Nothing happened!"

Duffy exploded. "Oh, really? That's really nice of you. You take a homicide witness for a shower after your partner's been shot? Are you out of your fucking mind? Are you having that much trouble getting dates or what?"

"I told him to take her there."

They turned to see Eddie walking out of the squad room, followed by Tommy Cullen. Eddie turned to Cullen, gesturing to Daphne, "Tommy, get her outta here."

Cullen took Daphne by the arm and led her away. Eddie then faced Duffy. "There was press all over the place. I didn't want her face on the news, so I told him to take her someplace quiet until things calmed down."

Duffy wasn't sure how to respond. "Oh, really?" he said.

"It was my decision," Eddie said. "Not his."

"Well, you see, I'm the deputy chief fire marshal," Duffy responded, "and every now and then I like to be included in decisions."

"I understand," Eddie said, trying to restore the big windbag's wounded pride. "In fact, after Jordy briefs me, you guys can take over the press conference. And you can take the lead case. How's that?"

"Yeah," Duffy said, suddenly liking Flemming's plan. He liked it a lot. "All right."

"I'm ready to be briefed, okay?" Eddie said to Jordy.

"Yeah," Jordy said.

"Excuse us," Eddie said to Duffy.

Duffy replied, "Yeah, sure," then glared at Jordy. "Beep me when you're ready for the press conference."

"Will do, Chief," Jordy answered.

"Are you ready to brief me?" Eddie asked Jordy, whisking him away, quickly.

"Yeah," Jordy repeated.

Eddie turned and started walking back to his office. Jordy trailed behind him, feeling more and more like he was Sancho Panza to Eddie's Don Quixote. Jordy sensed that Eddie Flemming was not pleased, and he had a pretty good idea of why. He said, "Eddie, I—"

Eddie turned to him, and his expression—sheer anger bubbling to the surface—silenced Jordy right away. "Wait," Eddie said.

They proceeded into the detective squad room. A bunch of the boys were kibitzing about drinking bad coffee. "Hey, fellas," Eddie said to them, "can you give us a few minutes, please? Thanks."

They filed out without question.

Jordy said, "Look, Eddie, just so you know—I didn't touch her."

"Well, maybe you should have," Eddie snapped, "because nobody's gonna believe you didn't . . . including me!"

"I took her there for a shower and that's it."

"Just a shower?" He gave Jordy a questioning look.

"Yeah—just her in the shower," Jordy said. "Nothing happened. Look, I'm sure you probably think I'm a fool and I fucked up, but—"

"No, I don't think you were a fool, I just think you were stupid about it," Eddie said. "I mean, to say the least, you oughta know better. You don't know her well enough. She's got the potential to fuckin' *hang* you—you know that? If she even suggests that you made a pass at her, it's fuckin' over. You can deny it all you want, it won't make a fuckin' bit of difference—you're dead."

"I told you," Jordy said. "I thought I was doing the right thing, you know. I think she's innocent."

"It's not up to you to decide whether she's innocent or not. Don't you understand—that's why you're a professional."

"Oh, c'mon," Jordy shot back. "Didn't you ever go out on a limb for somebody? I mean, you should've heard her there, tellin' her whole story. I believed her."

"How you go out on a limb for somebody is by giving her a number of an immigration lawyer," Eddie said. " 'Here, here's the number of an immigration lawyer'—that's how you help her. But you can't get involved with her like that. You're gonna jeopardize your career, you're gonna jeopardize your life, and you're gonna jeopardize my case. And let me give you another piece of advice: Maybe you don't watch TV, but I'm gonna let you in on a little secret—the whole fuckin' world watches television. And when you go out there, they know your face. And the little bit of fame, the little fuckin' itty-bitty piece of fame that I have in this fuckin' city makes my job a lot easier. And I get a lot more done because of it.''

Jordy digested this chunk of Eddie Flemming wisdom. He asked, ''So why'd you help me back there with the chief? Why'd you stand up for me like that?''

Eddie began rummaging through his desk, looking for something. ''I don't know,'' He said. ''I like you. You remind me of a puppy I used to have. He used to piss all over the carpet, but I still kept him.''

Eddie found what he was looking for—a Cuban cigar. He jammed it into his mouth and searched for a light. He heard a match flaring and looked up. Jordy was holding out an Ohio blue tip. Eddie leaned in and lit the Cuban, puffing away.

A homicide detective and a fire marshal, on the same side for a change. Who'd have thunk it?

* * *

Outside, the reporters clambered for any shred of info they could catch. A spokesman by the name of Whitaker, whose job it was to deal with the hungry press corp, came outside. The journalists knew him, and were throwing questions at him before he could even open his mouth to speak.

Finally, he said to them, "One at a time, please! We're looking for two white male suspects in their thirties. We believe them to be of an Eastern European nationality."

This served to whet their journalistic appetites even more, each one shouting louder than the other to be heard. This was one of the biggest stories to hit the Apple since Donald Trump had been mugged in broad daylight in front of the Trump Tower almost a year earlier. A cop beaten up and a fire marshal shot, plus Eddie Flemming on the scene, was a major news event.

About fifty feet from all the commotion, Eddie and Jordy slipped out a side entrance—designed specifically to avoid the press—and walked nonchalantly down the street.

Eddie was saying, "And that's another lesson—if you got nothing to say, don't waste their time"— meaning the press—"don't waste their time or yours. Let somebody else do that."

Jordy asked, "So, what's the plan now?"

Ah, the eagerness of youth. Eddie said to him, "Look, you're on the team, so I'll call you when something happens—but right now I gotta propose to my girlfriend."

"Really?" Jordy asked. "Congratulations."

"Well, don't congratulate me," Eddie said. "She hasn't said yes yet."

Jordy said, "Well, look—I still think there's something I could be doing in the meantime to help find these guys."

They came to Eddie's car. He pulled the door open and said to Jordy, "Go home and get some rest. Sometimes you can try too hard. Sometimes you have to go away in order to come back."

"Kinda like you did with that shot back there?" Jordy asked.

"That's right," Eddie said.

"I get it," Jordy said.

"Good," Eddie said, " 'cause you don't look like you get it."

"I get it."

"You sure you get it?" Eddie asked.

"I get it."

"You get it?" Eddie pushed a little harder.

"No, I get it," Jordy said. He handed the two-sided coin back to Eddie, adding, "Trust me, I get it."

Eddie looked at the coin as Jordy turned to walk away. Eddie said, "Why don't you keep it?" He flicked the coin back to Jordy, who caught it skillfully.

"Don't say I never gave you anything," Eddie said.

Eddie Flemming, through some very accommo-dating friends in New York City's cutthroat real es-tate racket, had managed to procure for himself a two-bedroom, two-bath apartment on East Seventy-ninth Street in a newly constructed high-rise that overlooked Midtown Manhattan, a breathtaking panorama. The rent was an unheard of $1000 a month, a quarter of what the place was worth on the open market. Eddie's friends asked for nothing in return for the astonishingly low rent except to keep an eye on things in the building, to act as sort of a troubleshooter to ensure that everything was on the up and up. But that was all—Eddie Flem-ming was a clean cop. Granted, he could afford to be, given the big bucks that often came with being a celebrity. But the word on the street was that Eddie was clean and always had been.

He'd risen fairly quickly through the department, though the early years had been ball busters. Straight out of the academy he'd been assigned to

the O-Six on East Fifth Street, one of the toughest
precincts south of Harlem and the Bronx. The O-Six
covered most of the insanity that went down east of
Second Avenue, to the area called Alphabet City—
Avenues A through D, between Houston and Four-
teenth Streets. Alphabet City was—and remained—
the epicenter of crime in a city that had plenty to
spare. Eddie had chased drug dealers over rooftops;
watched a fellow rookie named Boyle nearly blown
in half by two rounds from a sawed-off shotgun in
the hallway of a shit hole tenement on East Third,
fired by a homicidal crack dealer named Antoine
Butts.

Even as a foot cop, Eddie Flemming knew that
gaining the confidence of the good people of Alphabet City was worth its weight in gold. The stout
Puerto Rican mamas and the bodega owners knew
Eddie's face and liked what they saw. He gained
their confidence; in return, they gave him tips even
the toughest detectives in the O-Six only dreamed
about. The people trusted Eddie Flemming, and
Eddie didn't let them down. The nastiest drug king-
pins, motorcycle scum, and all-around badasses
made themselves scarce when Eddie Flemming was
pounding the beat.

He was photogenic, Eddie Flemming was, and
quick with the Bronx-Irish wit. Within two years,

Eddie was making page-six headlines in the *New York Post* for his exploits and his wryly observant comments about being a cop in New York City: "I been shot, I been stabbed, I was even ambushed by a gang of nine-year-olds on rollerblades who kicked the living shit outta me with hockey sticks. But what the hell—that's what I love about this job." Even the most hard-edged New Yorkers took Eddie Flemming to their hearts. He was one of them, an honest product of the mean streets he protected. He symbolized the best qualities of the Big Apple: tough, demanding, uncompromising, even sentimental. The media had a field day.

From there, it was a quick scramble up the ladder of the NYPD. A week after he had made detective, Eddie broke a case that propelled him to the front pages. A drifter from Texas named Daniel Ratski had slaughtered his live-in girlfriend, a topless dancer. Daniel Ratski boiled her dismembered body parts in a huge aluminum pot, making a thick, tasty concoction with vegetables and diced potatoes, which he later served to three dozen homeless men in a Bowery mission where he was a volunteer. Eddie told the press, "I may never touch my mother's Irish stew again." Eddie Flemming was great copy.

Then came the Stephen Geller case.

Stephen Geller was a nice boy, everyone in his hometown of Great Neck, Long Island, agreed. He was the only child of Sidney and Lorraine Geller and the heir to a chain of discount shoe stores throughout New York, New Jersey, and Connecticut. Sidney Geller had made millions selling cheap penny loafers manufactured in Taiwan. He was a shrewd, tough businessman.

Nobody was exactly sure why it happened. Stephen Geller was pursuing his master's degree in art at Columbia University, and was an honors student. One sunny Saturday afternoon, he walked into the Florsheim shoe store on Madison Avenue and Fifty-first and tried on one pair after another of expensive shoes—all penny loafers. It was near closing time. Maybe the clerks were rude; maybe the shoes were too tight. For whatever reason, Stephen Geller pulled out a Walther P99 pistol—he'd bought it from a gun dealer near school—and opened fire, killing three clerks instantly: Arnold Shuster, thirty-six, from Bensonhurst in Brooklyn and the father of two young children; Julius Alvin, forty-four, from Sunnyside in Queens; and Patrick Bestler, thirty-nine, from Cliffside Park, New Jersey. After that, Stephen Geller calmly pocketed the Walther and strolled out of the store onto Madison Avenue, disappearing into the crowd, leaving half a dozen pairs of unbought penny loafers scattered about.

It appeared to be a senseless, cold-blooded massacre that stunned New York City—indeed, most of the country. Robbery was quickly ruled out as a motive—no money had been taken. Detectives Eddie Flemming and Leon Jackson were assigned the case. For the next two weeks they canvassed the neighborhood, questioning the local merchants, until they had enough for a composite sketch of the killer. Between them, Eddie and Leon spent a total of 125 hours in shoe stores around the city, and scrutinized the credit card receipts of every pair of penny loafers sold.

Then they hit pay dirt. A young man, matching the description of the sketch, had two days earlier purchased a pair of penny loafers at a shoe store in Herald Square, across the street from Macy's. Less than three hours later, Eddie Flemming and Leon Jackson arrested Stephen Geller as he made his way across the Columbia campus on the way to his art history class.

As a result of his shrewd, tireless police work, Eddie Flemming became even more of a celebrity. He'd cracked one of the nastiest cases in years, and barely broken a sweat.

The newspapers came first, then the magazine

people and the book people in short order. It wasn't long before Hollywood sat up and took notice. Dozens of fast-talking hustlers wanted a piece of him, promising him the moon. Eddie Flemming took it all in stride, with an amused indifference, and New York loved him even more for it. Hollywood made a movie about him that played on HBO. It was a huge hit; the cable network ran it nine times in a month.

Eddie Flemming had arrived. Not since Eddie Egan, the detective who broke the infamous French Connection heroin case, had any member of the NYPD gained such notoriety. From the upper reaches of the Bronx to the tip of Far Rockaway, everyone knew Eddie Flemming.

At about eight p.m that evening, Eddie pulled his car into the garage underneath his building. He'd stopped on his way home in the flower district, on Sixth Avenue in the West Twenties, and purchased a big bouquet of roses. Nothing but the best for his Nicolette.

He took the elevator up and walked into his apartment and did what he always did—closed the door hard and locked it behind him. Old habits never die.

He grabbed the phone, punched buttons, and barked, "It's Flemming—anything turn up? They check the hospitals? Airports?" A pause. Then: "Yeah, I hit him. I fuckin' hit him. Look, we should be all over everywhere—with dogs, choppers, everything. These guys are from fuckin' Czechoslovakia!"

He looked at the flowers and decided the fucking Czechs could wait. He said, "I'll call you later."

The apartment was a little messy, but nothing that he couldn't live with. A fat Haitian woman named Serena, whom Eddie adored, came in once a week to shovel out the apartment. She was due tomorrow, in fact. Eddie carefully arranged the roses in a vase that he filled with water from the kitchen tap. When they looked perfect, he sat down and wrote on the small card, *Nicky, I love you. Will you marry me?* He stuck the card next to the ring box and went to get everything ready. Nicolette was due any minute. He went to the stereo and hit PLAY on the CD player. It was one of those CD things where you could put more than one disc in at a time, and they rotated all by themselves. From the speakers, Tom Jones blasted out "What's New, Pussycat?"

Definitely the wrong mood. Eddie hit the button again, and this time the first few notes of "Sunshine of Your Love" by Cream came belting out. Also wrong, he mused. He hit the button again, and a beautiful duet, sung in Greek, came on. It was *their* song, even if Eddie didn't know the Greek language. It didn't seem to matter. Now inspired, he poured himself a drink and went back to work on the card when a knock on the door interrupted him. He smiled. Nicolette, unlike most women he'd known, knew how to arrive on time. He liked that. Usually the doorman was supposed to announce all visitors, but on Eddie's instructions, Nicolette came and went as she pleased.

"Coming," he called out, and smoothed down his hair. His heart was pounding. It wasn't every day a man proposed to his lady.

He opened the door, wanting to throw his arms around Nicolette and drag her inside. He was shocked, then, to see that the hallway was empty.

"Nicky?" he called out. No one answered. He stepped out into the hallway, the drink still in his hand and walked down the hall toward the elevator. Was his true love playing games with him? Nicolette wasn't the playful hide-and-seek type. He walked all the way down to the two elevators that serviced his floor. The lights on both indicated that they were both on the lobby floor. Strange. There was no sign of human life anywhere on the floor. He heard a woman's laughter as a door closed somewhere. He walked back down the hall toward the opposite end, near the fire exit. No one there, either.

She might have run into either of the exit stairwells, but Eddie doubted it. He walked back to his apartment. He turned around one more time. There was a figure behind him, just out of his view. Eddie was startled, and he didn't startle easily. The stranger came closer; Eddie scrutinized him.

He entered his apartment and closed the door, locking it twice. It wasn't until he felt the cool lead pipe make contact with the back of his skull that he knew he'd fucked up big time.

Eddie Flemming, the finest of New York's finest, swam back up to consciousness, already ransacking his brain for the name of one of the ten million souls in New York City who had it in for him. He found himself handcuffed to one of the dining room chairs. When he was able to focus his eyes, he saw that the clock on the CD player read 8:27. He'd been out for almost twenty minutes.

He had a beauty of a headache, and he could feel the blood trickling down the left side of his face. Then he saw the little guy sitting in a chair, facing him. He was wearing a cheap suit and scuffed shoes. He needed a shave and the services of a competent dentist. Behind him stood a beast of a man who, in the best *Sixty Minutes* style, was videotaping Eddie as his smaller friend played Mike Wallace. He even had a light mounted on top of the video camera. The glare hurt Eddie's eyes. A video camera. Eddie started to remember, and tried hard not to panic.

The smaller guy was holding Eddie's watch, his gold shield, and the two hundred or so in cash he'd had in his wallet. He was also smoking one of Eddie's expensive Cuban cigars, which, for some crazy reason, enraged Eddie more than anything else. The duo had done a first-rate job of ransacking Eddie's apartment—all of his crap was strewn on the floor, and most of the furniture was overturned. The smaller guy was holding the card Eddie had just composed to Nicolette.

"So who is she?" the smaller man asked in heavily accented English.

Eddie glared at Emil and replied, "None of your fuckin' business."

"Who is Nicky?" Emil asked again.

Eddie answered by spitting in Emil's face. Emil didn't even flinch. Instead, he spit back. Eddie spit a second time, scoring a direct hit. Instead of getting angry, though, Emil just laughed. The sound was chilling.

"It's okay. You know what I need? I need your opinion," Emil said.

"You do, huh?" Eddie asked. "About what?"

Leaning forward in his chair, Emil said, "You see, they are going to make movie about me, too, Eddie. And write books."

Not bothering to keep the sarcasm out of his tone, Eddie asked, "Write books? What's your fuckin' accomplishment?"

"I kill someone famous," Emil replied. "And I saw you on the page of *People* magazine." When Eddie didn't reply, Emil said, "Good. Be tough to the end. Actor who plays you will want you to die like hero."

Eddie looked up at the video camera. The tall man was undoubtedly the big ox who'd filmed Leon getting the shit kicked out of him. Oleg returned Eddie's glare.

"Video—so tabloids don't have to do reenactments." Emil said, "They are going to have real movie this time."

Still squirming with the cuffs behind his back, Eddie said, "If you kill me and film it, you're putting a noose around your neck."

This pleased Emil for some reason. He started to

laugh again. Oleg joined in—Eddie, too. Emil turned to Oleg and ordered, "Turn it off."

Oleg obeyed. Emil turned back to his prisoner, saying, "No, we are insane. Who else but crazy men would film their murders?"

Film their murders. Eddie remembered the whore in the sleazy hotel.

Emil went on. "So we kill someone famous, and if we are caught, we are sent to mental hospital. But what good is money there? Because once in hospital, I say I not crazy. Just pretended to be acquitted. We see psychiatrists. They must certify we are sane, and because of your double-jeopardy law, we cannot be tried for same crime twice. We come out free, rich, and famous!"

"This is great idea!" Oleg chirped.

Unbelievable, Eddie thought. He shook his head. "You really think you'll be able to fool a jury with this bullshit? How fuckin' stupid are you?"

Emil laughed coldly once again. He took Eddie's pistol and smacked him across the face with it. Eddie saw lots of exploding colors and tried his best to stay conscious. If he went out, he was as good as dead. Emil whacked him again across the face for good measure, then put the barrel of the gun to Eddie's temple.

"Smarter than Americans," Emil said. "You're

fed crybaby talk shows all day long. Not only will Americans believe me, they will cry for me." He chuckled coldly and went on, "So, Detective Eddie Flemming, would you like to say good-bye to your Nicky? Maybe you can propose to her now, on the video."

Eddie said nothing, only glared at the little weasel who planned to get over on all of America.

Emil puffed impassively on one of Eddie's Cuban cigars. "Okay," he finally said to Oleg. "He has nothing to say. Give me a pillow. Give me a fucking pillow!"

The old pillow-over-the-head routine to muffle the sound, Eddie thought and squirmed. Oleg handed Emil the pillow. Emil then pressed it against Eddie's head, and said to his partner, "Start the camera."

Oleg said testily, "Cut! This is my project! I am the director. And *I* say action."

"Shut the fuck up!" Emil shouted. He looked at Eddie and rolled his eyes, as if to say, "See what I have to put up with?"

Oleg made a small production out of setting up the video camera just the way he wanted it before declaring, "And . . . action!"

Oleg started filming as Emil raised Eddie's service revolver. Out of gut instinct, Eddie kicked out at Emil's hand. The little prick was fast, though—Emil pulled away from Eddie's foot and backed out of his reach.

Emil raised the pistol again, aiming at Eddie's head. He cocked the hammer. In that split second, Eddie was up, standing as erectly as was possible under the circumstances. He charged Emil full-tilt, head-butting him in the face, knocking the scurvy little murderer flat on his bony ass. Emil's gun flew out of his hand and landed somewhere on the floor behind them. Without missing a beat, and still handcuffed to the chair, Eddie spun around and stabbed Oleg with the chair legs, backing him into the wall. Oleg gripped the video camera for dear life.

Emil was up now and working his way toward Eddie's gun, which in the confusion had tumbled to the floor. Using strength he didn't know he possessed, Eddie managed to stand up as best he could, and smacked Emil with the back of the chair he was still bound to—using his trapping as a weapon.

Emil fell to the floor with a loud *whoomph* sound, the wind knocked clear out of him. Eddie launched himself over toward Emil, still tied to the chair, and started jumping up and down on top of the sleazy little prick, stabbing him with the chair legs, two of which cracked and broke.

Oleg came at Eddie now. Eddie charged toward him, knocking the big Russian onto the couch. Seeing the gun still unclaimed on the floor, Eddie managed to position himself in such a way so that he tipped backward on the chair and landed on the gun. He grasped it in his hands—and what a fucking glorious feeling it was—and struggled to stand upright again. He fired and managed to hit a lamp shade, an expensive one he'd gotten at Bloomingdale's. He got off another shot, and this time hit the window blinds. They dropped from the left side of the window and clattered to the floor. Moonlight spilled into the room.

Eddie turned on his heels, feeling in control for the first time since these scumbags had invaded his home. He looked for his assailants, trying to get his bearings in the dark room. In that half second of disorientation, Eddie didn't see Emil charging at him again, didn't see the shiny object clenched in his fist.

He saw Emil's right hand shoot out at him and then pull back. Eddie looked down, saw the knife sticking out of his belly. He stumbled backward, staring down in mute disbelief. The gun slipped from his hand and dropped to the carpeted floor with a muffled thud.

Eddie dropped to his knees, the dark patch of

blood blooming on his shirt. Emil grabbed the pistol, while Oleg clambered for the video camera. He picked it up and knelt down next to Eddie and started filming a close-up.

Eddie dimly realized he was dying—the great Eddie Flemming was losing it. The pain was excruciating. He willed himself to stay conscious. He was Eddie Flemming, for Christ's sake, the pride of the NYPD, the boy from the Bronx who took shit from no one, certainly not a couple of low-life foreigners who'd been lucky enough to sleaze their way into his very home. He'd traded fire with the baddest of New York City's badasses. He'd survived situations the oddsmakers said were impossible for any cop, especially a rookie cop. He was a celebrity, a big shot. Jesus Christ, it wasn't supposed to end this way, a crappy kitchen knife buried in his gut, his lungs filling with his own blood.

Emil looked around the room, grabbing a black pillow from the couch. He pressed it down onto Eddie's face, finishing him off. Eddie kicked wildly, suffocating. He didn't give it up easily.

The last sound Eddie Flemming heard was from a Frank Sinatra CD, which was still playing. Frank was belting out, "You'd Be So . . . to Come Home to." A Cole Porter tune. Eddie had always loved

Cole Porter. As he sank into the throes of death, he saw Nicolette's face. It pained him even more that he wouldn't be around to tell her how much he loved her. He hoped she already knew.

TEN

Eddie Flemming's funeral was the biggest in New York City's memory.

Every off-duty member of the NYPD had showed up in full dress uniform, close to three thousand strong, to pay their respects to the one cop that virtually all of them aspired to be like. Every local politician had showed up, from the powerful Manhattan borough president to the lowliest assemblyman from Staten Island. News crews from as far away as Chicago and Detroit had come to cover the story. Hollywood's movie elite and New York's literary finest were there. Even in death, Eddie Flemming was a news event.

If a viewer in New York happened to tune into the local NBC affiliate, Channel 4, he would have seen one of the station anchorpersons, a chubby Puerto Rican anchorwoman named Luisa Torres, clutching a mike and reporting on the funeral. Eddie was being laid to rest in Calvary Cemetery in Queens, right off Exit 3 of the Long Island Expressway.

On television, Luisa Torres, looking solemn and somber, intoned, "Detective Flemming was one of the most decorated NYPD detectives in the history of New York. Among the several thousand arrests during his career—the famed Stephen Geller case. He was widely loved by the community in which he served. His partner, Leon Jackson, eulogized him." In the upper right-hand corner of the TV screen was a picture of Eddie Flemming from graduation day at the academy. Eddie was smiling brightly, but looked ready to kick any ass that gave him a bad time. It was a sad day indeed for the city of New York.

Leon Jackson appeared on-screen, dressed in his finest suit. He didn't look much worse for the wear from Emil's savage beating.

Oleg made sure to move in a little closer as he filmed the funeral off the TV set.

Leon said into Luisa Torres's microphone, "Eddie was my mentor, my best friend and my partner . . . He taught me the meaning of the word *cop*."

"Tragedy," Oleg noted with approval. "Every great film must have one."

On TV, Leon Jackson blinked back his tears and continued, "He was a man in every sense of the word. I'll miss him." Then Leon looked over at Eddie's coffin, where a half dozen NYPD SWAT boys wielded rifles, preparing to give Eddie the traditional twenty-one-gun salute. Leon said softly, "Sleep well, brother." He started chanting "Amazing Grace."

Oleg panned away from the television in the small hotel room, this one in a run-down dump called the Times Square Motor Lodge, on West Forty-fourth Street, and focused on the hustle and bustle of midday Times Square. He swung the camera back to Emil, who was sitting on the bed, pouring some clear liquid into an ashtray. He produced a very large hypodermic needle, which he carefully filled with the liquid. He took the full needle and inserted it into a lightbulb, filling it. He put the bulb down on the table—right next to a can of gasoline.

His fever had broken, the Russian noted, but he'd be walking with a limp for the foreseeable future.

The least Paulie Herman, proprietor of P. B. Herman's, could do was throw a traditional Irish wake for his late buddy.

It was an hour after the funeral, and his place was packed with cops of all ranks, along with prosecutors, city officials, and lawyers. The cops were all wearing black ribbons on their badges. Leon Jackson was there, knocking back a few. He was still in a daze; like the others, he just couldn't believe Eddie was gone.

Paulie had set out a first-rate buffet, as befitted the occasion. A throng of reporters clambered to get inside, but this wake was officially closed to the press corps. Paulie's manager, a burly Irishman named Sean Flannagan, was standing at the entrance, keeping the reporters at bay. He said to one aggressive reporter from the *Daily News*, "No means no! You want me to get ugly?"

None of them did. Flannagan's assistant, a Hispanic man named Jorge Colon, entered the fray, saying, "Gentlemen, we're sorry, but this is a private affair."

Leon sat alone at a table—Eddie's table. *Their* table. He was drinking a double scotch. Tommy Cullen made his way over to the table and pulled out a chair—Eddie's chair, as it turned out.

"Don't sit there," Leon mumbled.

Cullen understood immediately and took another seat. Jordy sat silently in the booth, fiddling with something in his palm. Declan Duffy sat down and slid a glass of scotch, straight up, over toward Jordy, while sipping a glass of his own. The two sat and drank in respectful silence. Looking up, Duffy saw a tear roll off Jordy's cheek. Jordy was staring at the coin he was turning over in his hand, back and forth, endlessly. It was a two-headed coin.

It was Eddie's two-headed coin. *Don't say I never gave you anything*, Eddie had said. Eddie, Jordy thought, you gave me a hell of a lot more.

Robert Hawkins came in dressed for the occasion in a crisp black suit, shaking hands all around. As a staunch defender of the NYPD, he was one of the only two journalists allowed inside. Nicolette Karas was sitting at another table, nursing her third scotch. Hawkins made straight for Leon, who stood. They embraced. Leon motioned to the table behind him. Hawkins sat beside Nicolette. She stared at him for what seemed like an eternity. It was clear that she was three sheets to the wind—completely bombed—and who could blame her?

She said to Hawkins, "He was going to propose to me. The crime-scene guys found a card he'd written out to me. And a ring box . . . those fuckers that killed him have my ring. They have my diamond engagement ring."

In a rare display of compassion, Hawkins touched Nicky's shoulder gently. "I know," he said.

Nicolette said to him sharply, "What do you

mean you know? He told you he was gonna propose to me?''

''Well, he—'' Hawkins started to say.

''I want to hear everything he said.''

''Well, that morning,'' Hawkins said, ''he was
talking to me and Leon about marriage.''

''Oh, my God,'' Nicolette said, suddenly realizing.
''We were having lunch here. He started making
overtures, talking about another pair of shoes in his
closet . . . but I got a call to anchor and I walked
out on him. I walked out on him when he was
trying to ask me to marry him!''

This brought on a fresh round of tears, mixed
with a lot of rage. She felt cheated. She went on,
''I'd never had a great relationship before. I'd never
made great choices with men. And he wasn't easy
to get to know. He was older. My parents told me
I was nuts to get involved with him, but he was so
great to me. Always encouraging, telling me I could
do anything.''

She took a sip of her drink and said, ''He was *the*
one. You know, I'd give up everything—everything—for just a little more time. I would've spent
fifteen minutes with him if that's all I knew I had.''

Maggie, Hawkins's producer, charged through
the crowd, clutching a cell phone. Trailing behind

her was her assistant, the chubby girl who always looked harried.

Maggie called out, "Robert, you've got a call. "Hold on—stay right there," she said into the phone. "Just stay where you are."

Hawkins was furious at her. Nodding in Nicolette's direction, he said, "Don't be ridiculous—can't you see I'm busy here?"

"Trust me," Maggie said, thrusting the cellular at him. "You're gonna want to take this call."

"Hang up the phone," Hawkins ordered her, "and go get yourself a drink."

"Take the call," Maggie said, and she meant business.

"Take the call," the assistant urgently repeated.

Hawkins sighed and faced Nicolette again. "Sorry."

She turned back to her drink. Hawkins said into the phone, "Hello, who is this?" He listened for a minute, his eyes growing wide, and said, "How do I know this is you?"

He shot out of the booth, pacing as he listened to whoever was at the other end of the line. "Where?" he then asked.

Emil was at a pay phone on the corner of Broadway and Fiftieth. As usual, Oleg was filming him. "Come to 45 Broadway. Don't bring the police.

Come alone or you'll be in my next film," Emil instructed.

"Look, asshole, I've been threatened by better than you," Hawkins said in a seethingly low tone.

"No," Emil countered. "I'm the best that's ever threatened you."

Hawkins believed him somehow. "You know what? They're gonna get you," he said.

"We'll talk about that," Emil said.

Getting excited now by the prospect of helping to apprehend Eddie Flemming's killer—not to mention the ratings grab that would go along with it— Hawkins said, "What about surrendering?"

"Four o'clock," Emil instructed. "Gives you time to go to bank. Three hundred thousand dollars." When Hawkins did not respond, Emil said, "Hey, asshole—are you still there?"

"Yeah, yeah, I'm here," Hawkins said. His mind was going in thirty directions at once. If this guy was on the level, the possibilities were sky-high. "But, look, the cash—it doesn't work that way."

Emil was getting angry at this TV big shot Robert Hawkins. No wonder everyone in America was fat and stupid—they watched shitheads like Robert Hawkins on the television all day long. "If you don't want my film, I will call another show. And *they* will show it," he said.

"All right," Hawkins said. "I'll meet you. I need two things from you. I want exclusivity, and you will surrender to me."

Emil's response was quick: "Bring cash."

Emil hung up before Hawkins could say anything more. Hawkins handed the phone back to Maggie, who was just as excited as he was. Forgetting Nicolette, he grabbed Maggie and began hustling for the door.

"Let's go."

At four o'clock on that same unseasonably warm afternoon, Jordy Warsaw and Deputy Chief Declan Duffy returned from Eddie Flemming's funeral, pulling up in a redcap on the street in front of Fire Station Nine-One. They were both wearing their shields on their uniforms, and each had a small black ribbon across it.

Upstairs, Bobby Korfin and Daphne were sitting at a table, drinking weak coffee when Jordy and Duffy walked in. Korfin's right arm was in a sling, and his side was heavily bandaged. He was lucky to be alive—unlike Eddie Flemming.

Seeing their faces, Korfin really didn't need to ask, but he did anyway. "How was it?"

"Not good," Jordy said, feeling dazed. He simply

could not grasp the notion that the great Eddie Flemming was dead.

Duffy, however, was all business. He turned to Korfin and asked, "Did the DA videotape her deposition?"

"Yeah," Korfin said. "He finished a while ago."

"All right. Go ahead and swing by her apartment. Let her pick up some clothes—then take her straight to Hoover Street. You got that?"

"Yes, sir," Korfin answered.

Duffy turned to leave, but didn't miss the look that passed from Jordy to Daphne—a look that to him seemed like one of budding love.

"Hey, Chief—mind if I take her?" Jordy asked.

Against his better judgment, Duffy said, "All right. But no water sports."

Jordy and Korfin escorted Daphne down to the street. Suddenly, a short, tubby man in a Hawaiian shirt and a Yankees cap ran up behind them and asked, "Excuse me—Jordan Warsaw?"

"Yeah, that's me," Jordy said.

"You Jordan Warsaw?" the man asked again. He was holding an official-looking envelope.

"Yeah," Jordy said.

The guy shoved the envelope into Jordy's hand and said, "Consider yourself served."

Jordy hoped that the envelope wasn't what he

thought it was. He ripped it open and pulled out some papers with a Manhattan court seal on the top. Daphne, curious, tried to read them.

"Daphne, could you come over to the car, please?" Korfin said. He tucked her into the backseat, then went back to Jordy and read over his shoulder.

Korfin asked, reading, "*Zwangendaba* is suing you, the department, and the city of New York for ten million? Who the hell is Zwangendaba?"

Jordy remembered, and then grew even more depressed. "The mugger. In the park."

First Eddie Flemming, now a nickel-and-dime street mugger named Zwangendaba. Jordy fought back the urge to break into tears. Some days it just didn't pay to get out of bed.

Emil and Oleg upgraded their living status—they were both comfortably ensconced in a very pleasant room at the Marriot Marquis on Forty-fourth and Broadway. The room was adorned with tacky hotel art and cheap plastic flowers—Emil and Oleg nonetheless thought it to be the height of luxury.

Robert Hawkins sat on the sofa, watching Oleg's video on the room TV. His mouth hung open; he was amazed and appalled at the same time. On the tape, Eddie was losing the fight in grainy black and white. The room was dark, but there was no mistaking it—these sick bastards had told the truth—they'd taped Eddie's murder. Worse—if anything could be worse—Oleg was *taping* Hawkins as he watched Eddie's killing on the television. They'd never prepared him for this at Columbia journalism school.

"Give me the money. Where is the money?" Hawkins heard Emil say behind him.

"It's here, it's here," Hawkins said, slamming a large briefcase on top of the television, then opened it. Inside was more cash than either Emil or Oleg had ever laid eyes on. "You wanna count it? It's all here. Now you'll give me the tape?"

"Be patient, partner," Emil said.

From behind the camera, Oleg reached out and yanked the handkerchief out of Hawkins's suit pocket. He wiped the sweat from Hawkins's brow daintily. Clutching the camera, Oleg brought himself into the frame and started hugging Hawkins, just another happy tourist. Oleg mugged for the camera. Hawkins looked both frightened and disgusted.

"Hard to believe? Watch!" Oleg, uncannily imitating Hawkins, announced.

*   *   *

They pulled up in front of her building, a shabby tenement walk-up on West 112th Street, in desperate need of some renovations. Jordy considered himself fortunate when he found a parking space only a few doors down the street—a minor miracle in the Big Apple. Together they entered the building—the front door lock was broken, making it easy for anyone to get inside the place, Jordy noted with some concern.

They made their way up the stairs to the third floor. Next to the door to Daphne's apartment sat a beautiful bouquet of roses, two dozen in all.

"What's this?" Jordy asked.

"I don't know," Daphne said puzzled. She plucked the card from the bouquet and read, "*Good luck with all your troubles. I'm here if you need me. Ludwig.*"

"Who is he, your boyfriend?" Jordy asked suspiciously.

"Ludwig? He's gay," Daphne said with a smile. "Are you jealous?"

"If I was your boyfriend, I might be," he said.

"If you were my boyfriend," Daphne said suddenly glum, "I'd suggest you find another girlfriend who isn't going to jail ten thousand miles away."

"A good immigration lawyer could stall the process," Jordy said. "Eddie recommended one."

The sexual tension between them was thicker than her grandmother's pea soup. Gazing into his eyes, Daphne said, "No matter what happens . . . I'm glad I met you."

"I'm glad I met you," Jordy said, and the dam blew wide open. They kissed, their passion growing until they were interrupted by a tenant coming up the stairs.

"We better get your stuff," he said.

Daphne looked disappointed, but said nothing. Jordy unlocked the door and went in first. Daphne followed him in, holding the bouquet of roses, which she placed on the table in the tiny, cramped kitchen. She turned back to Jordy, and they stood looking at each other for a moment, their faces close. They kissed again.

They broke apart, reluctantly, Jordy saying, "You better get packed."

"Right."

"Maybe I'll make some coffee," Jordy suggested.

"It's over the stove," Daphne yelled, heading off through the small living room. Jordy looked around the small kitchen. It was your standard New York City tenement kitchen, with barely enough room to turn around in.

Daphne headed off down the narrow hall, saying,

"I'll get my clothes." Adjacent to the tiny bathroom was a small closet.

As with most apartments in Manhattan, this one was dark. Jordy flipped the light switch.

There was a blinding flash of light and a loud popping noise, like a shot being fired. The lightbulb exploded, setting the ceiling on fire and releasing a rain of flames into the apartment. Jordy jumped back instinctively as Daphne came charging back into the room.

"Get back!" he shouted to her, more surprised than shaken. This was a fire, and he knew the drill. Pushing Daphne away, he noticed a fire extinguisher sitting in the corner. Smart of Daphne to keep one on hand, Jordy thought, already reaching for it. The fire continued spreading throughout the small kitchen; the walls and the ceiling both erupted in flames now.

Jordy grabbed the extinguisher and aimed it at the flames licking the kitchen walls and ceiling. As he pressed the handle, Daphne cried out, "No! That's not mine—!"

Jordy let loose with a stream of liquid he realized too late was gasoline. Instead of putting out the fire, the extinguisher fed it a seven-course meal. A searing ball of flame engulfed the kitchen, blinding them both momentarily. He tried to turn the damn thing off, but the handle locked up on him. In a split second, the flames raced across the floor and engulfed the extinguisher, burning Jordy's hand to a second-degree crisp in an instant.

He wailed in agony and flung the fire extinguisher into the kitchen, then slammed the warped wooden door shut, knowing the damn thing was going to blow any second. He whipped off his sports jacket and stuffed it under the bottom of the door, hoping he could block the smoke long enough for them to escape.

He turned and saw Daphne wielding one of the chairs, looking like a crazed interior decorator, about to smash it through the rusty-gated living room window.

Jordy knew it would be a big, big mistake.

"No! Don't do it!" he cried out, but he was about half a second too late. The chair flew through the window, shattering glass outward and letting the chilly afternoon air inside. Then the world exploded.

A deafening roar and flesh-cooking flames and heat filled the room. Jordy dived out of the way, grabbing Daphne and knocking her to the floor. He covered her body with his as smoke and fire jettisoned across the ceiling, flash-frying the furniture.

He pulled her up and pushed her down the hallway to the bedroom. A window over the bed faced the fire escape. The window was covered by a rusty gate, not surprisingly. Fire escapes and gated windows went hand in hand in New York. Together they clawed at it. "It's locked," Daphne said.

"Where's the key?" Jordy asked, the pain in his hand starting to blossom.

"It's not mine!" Daphne cried, starting to panic. "I—"

"Okay, get in the bathroom! Now!" Jordy urged.

He pulled out his cellular and hit the speed dial. He yelled, "Ten-seventy-five, ten-seventy-five! Twenty-seventy and Eighth, all right? We're trapped—two alarms on arrival, and haul ass!"

He clicked off. Smoke was cascading into the bedroom, mostly from under the door. These old buildings burned like paper. He yanked a down comforter off the bed and shoved it under the doorjamb, which helped keep the smoke out, but not enough.

Jordy then pulled Daphne into the bathroom. It was a tight squeeze. Jordy slammed the door shut, then ran his singed hand under the cold water. There was a tiny window next to the sink—Daphne looked out and thought she heard the sirens. She tried to open it, until Jordy said, "Don't open the window—it'll suck the fire toward us!"

Jordy wrapped his hand in a towel as Daphne cried out, "It's nailed down! Oh, my God, it's nailed down!"

And so it was. Two nails had been hastily pounded into the windowframe. And on top of one bent nail was an unusual object—an NYPD gold shield.

"They were here!" Daphne wailed.

"Jesus Christ," Jordy said. "That's Eddie's."

"They were here!" Daphne screamed again, and sounded as if she were on the verge of total hysteria, undiluted panic fraying her nerves. The butchers had been in her home, in her bedroom and her bathroom.

"Calm down, Daphne," Jordy said. They were precious seconds away from being barbecued alive. The odds of beating this one would've gotten *bupkis* from the neighborhood bookmakers. Jordy tried to calm Daphne down by saying, "Just get in the bathtub and calm down!"

Daphne pulled back the shower curtain. Sitting in the tub was a ten-gallon can, and it wasn't body lotion.

"It's gasoline," Daphne said.

"What?" Jordy asked, not believing their crappy luck. A can of high octane—the icing on the fucking cake. It was a bomb waiting to go off. Daphne tried pouring it down the bathtub drain, which was—not surprisingly—stopped up, forming a little puddle of gas. Jordy grabbed the can and tried pouring it down the sink drain, with the same results.

"Jesus Christ! It's clogged, goddamn it!" The pricks had done a beautiful job—they had thought of everything.

"Do something, please," Daphne begged, her panic rising like mercury in August. "We're going to die!"

That was a distinct possibility. The fire outside the bathroom was raging, the bathroom's wooden door beginning to smoke and burn. They were trapped. The whole place would explode again as soon as the flames licked the gasoline in the sink and bathroom. Jordy poured the rest of the can into the toilet, the old-fashioned kind with a pull chain and a water box on a wooden shelf seven feet up. His grandmother's apartment in Queens had one just like this. Jordy tossed the empty can aside and gave the chain a hefty yank. It broke off in his hands. Yes indeed, they'd thought of *everything*.

"Forget it, forget it," Jordy said. "Just stay low and stay calm. *Just stay low!*"

They were toast, and he knew it. No way would the smoke-eaters get there in time. Then he spotted the exposed water pipe that ran up the wall to the ceiling, next to the water tank. As quickly as he saw it, Jordy made his decision. He grabbed the copper water pipe, about two inches around, and jamming his feet against the wall for leverage, he pulled with every drop of strength he had to break it loose. It creaked a little, but didn't give much. He yanked again, sweat pouring off his face, the tendons in his neck bulging hideously with the effort.

He heard the sirens in the distance, and silently prayed for a miracle.

At the same moment, from an apartment rooftop across the street, Oleg Razgul was videotaping the fire. Smoke was pouring out of the second- and third-floor windows now, thick and black and carrying the stench of rotted wood. Oleg turned the video camera on himself, as the first three fire engines roared up Eighth Avenue.

He said, "Fire marshal is here. Everything is so messy. Everything is so crazy here. Look at this fire. Ninety percent of people who die in fires die from breathing smoke. So most likely they all die from eating smoke." He panned over to Emil and said, "But let me introduce you to my partner, and the man who started the fire. Say something to your fans, Emil."

He panned the camera over to the Czech, who

was calmly watching the fire rage, resting his arms on the ledge of the rooftop.

Emil blew a kiss to the lens of the video camera, then turned back to watch the spectacle. It was a shame to have to kill such a lovely creature as Daphne Handlova. He'd liked her; she'd have made a good wife. But love and sex would have to wait—such was the life of a criminal.

The smoke in the bathroom was so thick now, Jordy and Daphne could barely see each other. She was helping him now with the pipe. Together they pulled, knowing it was their last hope. Miraculously, the pipe finally ripped away from the wall and broke into a couple of long pieces, spraying gallons of cold water all over the bathroom, soaking the walls. Jordy managed to bend the pipe at the floor level enough so that the gushing water at the bathroom door drenched the flames that were licking the cracks in the door. He and Daphne were sopping wet and, unfortunately, still trapped by the fire that continued to rage on the other side of the bathroom door.

Jordy kept dousing the door, and said, "This'll at least buy us some time."

The water pressure in the severed pipe soon trickled down to a dribble. Jordy had one more trick up his sleeve, and it was a long shot. He grabbed a three-foot piece of broken pipe and, wielding it like a Louisville Slugger, smashed it against the bathroom wall a foot above the toilet. He smashed it a second time, then a third, until there was a hole in the wall that revealed the bathroom in the apartment next door. The old Sheetrock gave away easily, huge chunks crumbling away with each blow. At least the smoke had someplace to go now, instead of into their lungs.

Jordy peered inside. A little boy, maybe six or seven years old, was standing in the opposite bathroom, clutching a Bugs Bunny stuffed toy and looking understandably terrified. "What the hell!" Jordy said, then screamed at the kid, "Stay back, stay back!"

On the neighboring rooftop, Oleg filmed away, loving the footage he was getting. He said happily, "This is great film! You can see fire right now. And Daphne is in the fire."

Oleg Razgul and Emil Slovak, sort of a psychopathic Abbott and Costello, watched the building burn out of control. Oleg, as might be expected, was videotaping.

The little boy was crying hysterically, screaming in Russian, "The hallway is on fire! Help me!"

"Tell him it's okay," Jordy said to Daphne, dimly wondering where the hell the kid's parents were.

He kept pounding at the wall with the pipe. When the hole looked big enough, he tried pushing Daphne through it just as the bathroom door burst into flames.

"Come on, we gotta go!" he hollered, forcing her through the jagged hole in the wall. In precious seconds the entire room would incinerate. When Daphne was through, Jordy moved to climb through after her. Looking back he saw Eddie's badge on the windowsill. He snatched it off the nail and dropped it into his pocket, then scrambled through the hole.

When the bathroom finally exploded, blowing out chunks of glass and wood onto Twenty-seventh Street, Oleg caught it all on tape. The fire engines had finally arrived. Men were jumping off trucks and dragging hoses, connecting them to every available fire hydrant on the street. Tenants poured out of the building, carrying whatever they could grab—cats, dogs, parakeets, clothes, and personal belongings. The street filled up with gawkers; the firefighters tried to keep them back until the cops arrived.

Korfin and Garcia pulled up in a redcap just as Jordy, holding the little boy under one arm and dragging Daphne with the other, tore ass out of the burning tenement. A fireman was right there, grabbing the kid, while another came up and grabbed Daphne.

"Get 'em some oxygen!" Jordy said.

Korfin and Garcia ran over to Jordy and guided him over to a paramedic. His face was redder than a plum tomato; black crud ran from his nose. "Jordy—you all right, man?" Garcia asked.

"What the hell happened up there?" Korfin asked.

"It was a setup," Jordy explained, trying to catch his breath. "Somebody booby-trapped the apartment."

"Who?" Korfin asked. "Who booby-trapped it?"

"Gotta be the same guys," Jordy said as the paramedic cleaned and bandaged Jordy's burned hand, a temporary measure at best.

"Are you burned anywhere else?" the paramedic asked.

"No, no, it's all right. I found this up there," Jordy said to Korfin and Garcia, showing them Eddie's shield. He spotted Daphne standing on the corner and yelled to anyone within earshot, "Get her some oxygen, dammit!"

A voice, one that sounded all too familiar, echoed through the throng clogging Twenty-seventh Street: "Isn't she gorgeous? She's my fire!"

They turned their attention to a deranged-looking

street person, one they knew all too well—Max Gornick, the attention-grabbing pyromaniac and all-around fire department groupie. Max was screaming now, "She's my fire! Me, Max Gornick! Arrest me! Arrest me! She's my fire!"

A news crew had arrived by this time. Max Gornick was screaming into a news camera, "I did this! Me, I did this! I'm Max Gornick!"

Jordy grabbed Max and pushed him roughly away, where he bounced off a couple of firefighters. Jordy barked, "Check out the crowd. They might still be here. Garcia, look around. Maybe you'll see something."

Jordy scanned the neighboring rooftops, which were all empty, while Bobby Korfin scanned the crowd. He came up blank. They could both hear Deputy Chief Declan Duffy bellowing into his cell phone, covering one ear to block out the din on the street: "You gotta speak louder! I can't hear you!"

Duffy turned and saw Jordy and his bandaged hand and asked, "Jesus Christ, Jordy—are you hurt? Are you all right?" He screamed into the phone again: "No, you have to speak up! What the hell . . . that's insane! What the hell are you talking about?"

"What is it?" Jordy asked. "*What is it?*"

Duffy clicked off and told Jordy, who let out a

string of profanities and hopped into the nearest redcap and took off up Eighth Avenue, heading uptown. If what Duffy said to him was true, there was gonna be hell to pay, and heads were gonna roll up and down Broadway.

Five minutes later, he pulled up in front of the UBN station headquarters on Columbus Avenue, screeching to a halt and taking half an inch of rubber off the tires. Forty floors above, the *Top Story* studio facade was lit up with thousands of lightbulbs, highlighted by the face of the one and only Robert Hawkins.

Oh, yeah. There would be some serious hell to pay this night.

ELEVEN

UBN, the United Broadcasting Network, was at that very moment the eye of the storm, even more than usual. The lobby was seven deep in angry off-duty cops from precincts all over the five boroughs of New York City. Leading the pack were Leon Jackson and Tommy Cullen, who were still in their black funeral suits. The lobby was bedlam. A couple of minimum-wage security guards cowered in the face of almost a hundred of New York's finest.

Behind the reception desk, Maggie, the *Top Story* producer, was trying in vain to calm them down. Her harried assistant, looking even more harried than usual—indeed, she looked terrified—was barking into the phone. "We have a disturbance in the lobby! Get security down here right now!"

Maggie was busy trying to explain to Leon Jackson, "I told you, he's not on the premises."

"And for the third time," Leon said, and he meant every word, "go get that tape and bring it here right now!" The city would have his balls for what he was doing, but he didn't give a shit.

"Any requests for that videotape have to go to *Top Story*'s attorney, Bruce Cutler," Maggie told him. "I'll be happy to give you the number."

"Lady, if you put Eddie's murder on TV, I'll get a warrant for your arrest and shove it so far up your ass it'll come outta your mouth!"

Maggie was not about to be intimidated, yelling back, "I want your shield number!"

A bunch of big-screen TV sets were mounted to the walls all over the room. From them, the voice of Robert Hawkins announced, "Viewer discretion advised!"

Maggie cried, "You want the tape?" She pointed to the television mounted on the wall in the office. "There it is!"

They turned their attention to the TV set. The *Top Story* logo flashed on the screen, with accompanying music. Robert Hawkins, looking grim, but with every hair neatly in place, sat behind his desk.

Hawkins said, "What we are about to broadcast is very graphic footage . . ."

Everyone in the room was riveted to the TV screen. Jordy noticed something going down outside on the street. A news van had pulled up and was idling at the curb. Robert Hawkins materialized out of the night and hopped into the van. His show had obviously been taped earlier that evening.

The van sped away down Amsterdam Avenue. Jordy hopped into the redcap, following them.

In the space of just a few hours, Emil Slovak and Oleg Razgul had graduated from eating at Hamburger Heaven to dining in splendor at Planet Hollywood on West Fifty-seventh Street, a chain of tourist traps once owned in part by movie stars like Bruce Willis and Arnold Schwarzenegger. They sat at a corner table, having just polished off a sumptuous meal.

Oleg videotaped the waiter uncorking a bottle of Cristal champagne—$200 in your neighborhood liquor store. Inside Planet Hollywood, it was marked up to $200 a bottle. The waiter poured them each a glass, then nodded at them and left. Typical Eurotrash, he thought.

Emil raised his glass, in a good mood now, and said into the camera, "America! Who says you cannot be success in America? I came here with nothing, knowing nobody. Now look!" He giggled maniacally. "I am success story!"

Oleg lowered the video camera, shutting it off. He asked Emil suspiciously, "*You* are success story? *I* am success story. Why do you say *I*? It should be *we*."

Emil gestured toward the huge wide-screen television set, where Robert Hawkins was doing the *Top Story* introduction.

"Good evening," he intoned with that brand of self-righteousness that made half of America love him and the other half want to knock his teeth down his skinny gullet. "Welcome to *Top Story*. Tonight I present tc you material of a graphic and violent nature never before seen on television. And I do so with a heavy heart. You will be a firsthand witness to the slaying of celebrated New York City homicide detective Eddie Flemming. It would be only normal to ask why. Why are we showing something so disturbing? And my answer is, as a journalist, I *must* show it. A democracy survives through the freedom of its media, and if we cannot see what is happening, then we don't deserve our democracy or our freedom. Eddie Flemming was my friend. I cried when I watched this footage and vowed to fight this violence with every molecule of my being from this day onward. Hopefully, this will have a similar effect on you. One final word: this material is absolutely not appropriate for children."

"Don't be paranoid," Emil said to Oleg. "You got one hundred fifty thousand dollars, didn't you?" True to his word, Robert Hawkins had come through with the cash. Emil went on, "I gave you half of what they gave me."

The tourists in Planet Hollywood started buzzing with excitement. Emil checked his watch.

"In movie they make of us, who do you think should act me?" Oleg asked.

"The one who got caught in the bathroom. George Michael," Emil said, humorously.

"I'm serious," Oleg said.

"Shut up," Emil said. "Look!"

The scene cut to Oleg's video footage. Eddie was handcuffed and bound to the chair. The light illuminated his face. Oleg, Emil had to admit, had indeed done a very professional job.

Oleg's voice came on the TV, though the camera was still on Eddie. Oleg was saying, "This is my project! I say action. I am the director! You are the talent. You wait for me to say action." Then: "Action!"

Then they could hear Emil saying, "Bad last moment. I cut it out."

Emil looked at Oleg, furious. He said, "I told you to cut that out before we handed in the tape!"

"Be quiet," Oleg snapped. "Watch."

As the video rolled on the huge television, a horrified silence fell over everyone inside Planet Hollywood. Customers, waiters, busboys—even the kitchen staff came out to watch the incredible footage being broadcast from sea to shining sea.

And there it was. On the screen, Emil was raising the pistol to Eddie's temple. Eddie pushed him over the desk, then wielded the chair and brought it down onto Emil, who fell off the desk and onto the floor. Eddie kept swinging the chair, driving Oleg back across the room—the picture quality got dizzying at this point, Oleg trying to fend off the blows and keep the camera steady at the same time. Eddie and Emil both went for the gun; Eddie knocked it out of Emil's way. Then Eddie was stabbing Emil with the legs of the chair, Emil rolling into a little ball on the floor. At that point Oleg came at Eddie, who knocked him over the coffee table and onto the sofa. The blinds and the lamp shade got shot to pieces, bathing the room with more light.

Then the world was treated to the sight of Emil stabbing Eddie in the stomach in graphic close-up, Emil crying, "Die! Die!"

Oleg beamed approvingly. Frank Capra would be proud.

Thirteen blocks to the south, in the heart of Times Square, Jordy followed the network van that carried Robert Hawkins and his crew. At the intersection of Forty-fourth and Broadway, Jordy, along with thousands of others, watched in stunned amazement as the video of Eddie's murder was splashed across the massive JumboTron screen, the same one used for the New Year's Eve countdown. Locals and tourists alike gaped at the spectacle of a taped murder, the ultimate TV taboo in the process of being shattered. Whether they were aware of it or not, broadcasting history was being made tonight.

Back inside Planet Hollywood, knives and forks hung suspended over plates as people watched Eddie Flemming's merciless slaughter unfold on national TV. Emil asked Oleg indignantly, "Why did you leave that stuff about you being a director?"

"Because I *am* the director," Oleg shot back. "Don't you fucking realize, if it wasn't for my film, for my talent, my idea to do this—no way would we be sitting here right now."

"Your idea?" Emil asked, clearly irritated. "I thought it was my idea."

Oleg bristled at Emil's words, his face turning the color of pickled beets. Emil didn't help matters any when he asked, laughing, "Aren't you just the cameraman?"

Oleg failed to see any humor. "Don't you realize this is fucking great American movie?" he said to Emil. "Watch the screen. Watch everybody here."

It was not difficult to see the effect Oleg's epic was having; everyone in the joint was glued to the television screen as Eddie Flemming fought valiantly against his two barbaric attackers. Emil watched the people watch him kill the big-shot New York detective. He heard Oleg say, "This is what America wants. Violence and sex—and I want my credit!"

Emil turned to Oleg and asked, "Credit?"

"Yes," Oleg said hotly. "Before we hand in the next video, I'm going to put titles on it—do you understand me? And I want my credit to read, 'Directed by Oleg Razgul.'"

"There is only one problem: you want credit, but I do not *share* credit," Emil replied.

Oleg was fuming. It was potentially dangerous to

anger the hulking simpleton, but Emil didn't seem to care. He pressed on. "You got that? You think you are a director? No! You're just a little, small Russian piece of shit! And I hate you! I fucking hate you!"

For good measure, Emil slapped Oleg hard across the face, just to show him who was boss. Oleg shot out of his chair and grabbed his steak knife. Emil pulled his gun—Eddie's gun. Just as Emil pulled the trigger, Oleg slammed the knife into Emil's arm.

Emil's shot went wild, ricocheting into a wall fixture. Chaos erupted inside Planet Hollywood. Women started screaming, waiters and busboys dived for cover under tables, and the smarter patrons bolted for the nearest exit. Oleg was sprinting through the restaurant like an Olympic runner doing the fifty-yard dash, clutching the video camera. He collided with a skinny waiter, sending him careening into a glass display that featured a life-size statue of Sylvester Stallone—once a principal Planet Hollywood backer—as Rocky Balboa. The sounds of shattering glass only added to the pandemonium, as people jammed the exits.

Pushing through the screaming, panicked patrons, Robert Hawkins appeared, trailed as usual by his camera crew. Behind them was a stocky, tough-looking man in an expensive Italian suit. Hawkins strode up to Emil and announced, "All right. I'm here."

Gaping at the knife stuck deeply in Emil's arm, Hawkins cursed, "Oh, Jesus." The horror of the knife wound explained the panic that gripped the people inside Planet Hollywood.

Emil yanked the knife out of his arm with nary a flinch. He tossed it aside and picked up a napkin to press against his wound. Hawkins thought it best to push forward. He introduced the well-dressed man with the bulldog jaw to Emil. "This is the man I told you about—this is Bruce Cutler."

The name meant nothing to Emil, an out-of-towner. But Bruce Cutler was a star to the people of New York, A fearless, tenacious, take-no-prisoners defense attorney, the Brooklyn-born Cutler had twice successfully defended John Gotti—the jewel in the Mafia crown—on murder and racketeering charges. Being grilled by Bruce Cutler on a witness stand was akin to being burned at the stake; Bruce ranted and raved, Bruce bullied and intimidated, and Bruce hammered it home until even the toughest, most street-hard stool pigeons caved in and recanted their own testimony. Cutler's courtroom histrionics earned the wrath of judges and prosecutors, but his clients always seemed to beat even the toughest raps—and New York loved him for it, the same way they had loved Eddie Flemming.

Simple and to the point, Emil greeted Bruce Cutler with, "Hi. I am Emil. I am insane. Are you my lawyer?" His blood seeped through the napkin.

"I'm not your lawyer until I see the money," Cutler said. Though John Gotti was one of the toughest criminals since Lucky Luciano and Frank Costello, he was at least sane. Cutler wasn't so certain about this Czech.

"I have your money," Emil said, picking up the briefcase and handing it to Cutler.

Bruce Cutler looked inside and saw mounds of cash. Glancing around suddenly, Emil started pushing plates and silverware aside on the table, frantically looking for something. Still holding the gun, Emil dropped to his knees and crawled under the table, throwing chairs aside.

"Where is it?" Emil shouted. "Shit! Where is it?"

If the man was planning on copping an insanity plea, Cutler mused, he was home free. Cutler said, "Take it easy, Emil. Stay with me. Sit down. What do you need? What are you looking for?"

Emil yammered desperately, "He has the camera! He got the movie!"

Trying to calm him down, as he had soothed the

volcanic temper of John Gotti, Cutler said, "Let's sit down and talk about it."

Emil continued his erratic search, already knowing it was fruitless. Neither he nor Cutler nor Hawkins noticed Jordy bull his way through the restaurant, his gun raised. He yelled at Emil, "Don't move! Don't move! Get your hands up! Drop the gun!"

Emil stood and dropped the pistol, then put his hands up. "I give up," he said.

Cutler said, "This man is unarmed, officer. He's surrendered."

Jordy's finger wavered on the trigger, wishing that Emil would make a threatening move. He had hoped to blast the little shitbox into the middle of next week. As a consolation prize, Jordy cracked Emil across the face hard, knocking him flat.

"What are you hitting him for?" Cutler said, suddenly concerned.

Jordy recognized Cutler but ignored him, concentrating on handcuffing Emil. He said to the cameraman, "Turn that camera off!"

Emil turned to the camera, playing up the sympathy angle by appearing to be more hurt than he was. He yelled to the cameraman Crimp, "No! Keep filming—"

Jordy realized just how media savvy Eddie's

killer was proving himself to be. He understood in that moment why Emil had surrendered without so much as a blink of the eye. Though Crimp's camera was still grinding away, Jordy yanked Emil by the cuffs and dragged him across the restaurant floor. Emil stumbled along, favoring his uninjured ankle a little more than necessary for effect.

"Don't say anything!" Cutler said to his client.

"Where are we going?" Emil asked.

Cutler was on his feet and scurrying to Emil's side. "I'm coming with you."

"Yes, yes, come with me!" Emil begged, playing the victim.

Cutler scurried to catch up with them, shouting after Jordy, "I'm invoking rights. I'm going with you down there, Emil."

The *Top Story* crew swarmed over Emil, Jordy, and Cutler, getting everything on tape. Cutler stayed close to Emil, making certain he was in the frame. Hawkins was ecstatic; this story was turning out better than anyone could have hoped for. His ratings would blow sky-high, and earn him Emmys, accolades—and a ton of cash.

By the time Jordy half-dragged a badly limping Emil out onto Fifty-seventh Street, New York's finest were pulling up, sirens screaming. Leon Jackson, accompanied by Tommy Cullen and another detective, Phil Murphy, jumped out of an unmarked car just as Jordy was loading Emil into his redcap. Leon ran over and grabbed Emil by the arm.

"Oh, no," Leon said. "I'll take him."

"No way!" Jordy said, pulling Emil back. "He's *mine!*"

"We're taking him," Leon argued, yanking Emil's arm. He felt like a chicken wishbone. "Don't argue with me!"

"He's my collar!" Jordy yelled.

"He killed my partner!" Leon shouted back.

"He's yours but I take him in," Jordy informed Leon. "I'll drive him to the precinct. You can have him, but I'm walkin' him in."

Leon looked at the news cameras that were filming their every word. Jordy *wanted* to be seen on TV taking Emil into custody—it was as simple as that. Jordy had caught the fever of the spotlight. Leon, having worked with Eddie for so long, could see it in his eyes.

"Okay, kid," Leon said to him. "Have your fifteen minutes." He turned to Cullen. "Tommy, ride with him."

Leon stared at Emil with more hatred than he'd felt for any criminal in his years as a detective, and he'd seen some doozies—thieves, murderers, rapists, child molesters; the list was endless. He and

Cullen and Jordy were trying to cram Emil into the backseat of the redcap, and not gently. He wasn't going easy, demanding his lawyer and playing the victim for the TV cameras.

Leon hissed at Emil, "You're goin' down, motherfucker, you are going down. I'll be there with a smile when they put you down!"

"Don't say a word!" Cutler pressed Emil "Don't respond to his taunting." He turned to Leon. "He's represented by council. You want to speak to someone, you speak to me!'

Tommy, going for the car door, pushed Cutler aside, saying, "Out of the way, Counselor."

"Don't you put your hands on me, Detective," Cutler said defiantly. He knew cops, probably better than anyone in the city.

Jordy pushed Emil into the backseat and slammed the door. Leon turned to Hawkins, whose camera crew was still filming and said, "And you— you'll pay for what you did!"

In a low tone Hawkins defended himself. "This footage will work in your favor. When the jury sees this—no matter what Cutler tries—they'll convict him."

"You oughta be ashamed. Ashamed of yourself." Leon looked disdainfully at Hawkins—the man had been his friend not two days ago.

"If I didn't put it on, somebody else would. I was Eddie's friend!" Hawkins said self-righteously.

"Don't give me that fucking shit," Leon said hotly.

Murphy nudged Leon, looking at the rolling cameras, and cautioned, "Don't get into it on TV."

Leon shouted, "All right—let's get going."

The rest of the cops went for their cruisers. In the midst of the insanity, with Emil securely tucked into the backseat, Jordy started the car, threw it into gear, and peeled off down Columbus Avenue. Leon and Hawkins were still screaming at each other, but at the sound of Jordy burning rubber, Leon and the other cops rushed to their unmarked cars. Leon knew what Jordy had on his mind, and it wasn't a pretty picture.

Jordy, his expression grim, tore down Ninth Avenue and hung a hard right onto West Fifty-seventh Street, running every traffic light that had the bad judgment to turn red. He turned north on the West Side Highway, heading uptown at eighty miles per hour like a man possessed, dodging taxis and weaving around minivans.

"Where are you goin', man?" Tommy Cullen asked nervously. "You're gonna lose everybody!"

Jordy ignored him, checking out Emil in the rearview mirror. Emil grinned back at him, not looking the least bit concerned or even remotely frightened.

We'll see about that, Jordy thought.

"This isn't the way to the station," Jordy dimly heard Tommy Cullen say. Jordy continued ignoring him, speeding uptown on the West Side Highway.

TWELVE

Jordy pulled off the West Side Highway and onto 130th Street, a deserted block surrounded by vacant buildings, warehouses, and utility shacks. There was not a human being to be seen anywhere.

Jordy slowed the car, looking for the most secluded spot. He found one that was perfect—a deserted, crumbling warehouse. He slammed on the brakes and stopped the car. It was slowly dawning on Tommy Cullen what Jordy intended to do. And if it came to pass, Tommy would be viewed as an accessory after the fact in the eyes of the law.

Jordy got out of the car. The bright lights of the George Washington Bridge glittered in the distance, two miles to the north.

"Jordy, what the hell—" Cullen started to say, climbing out of the car.

"What's going on?" Emil asked, no longer grinning.

Jordy yanked Emil hard out of the backseat. "Jordy, hold on, wait. What is wrong with you, man?" Tommy Cullen said.

Jordy was not going to be denied his revenge. He dragged Emil into the warehouse. Tommy Cullen helped, against his better judgment, protesting all the way: "Jordy—we can't do this, man! Would you listen, please?"

Jordy ignored young Tommy Cullen. He slammed Emil up against a wall and demanded, "Were you a fireman? How'd you know how to rig that apartment?"

"My father was fireman," Emil said. "He taught me about fire. Now it's my friend."

His fists still gripping Emil tightly, Jordy turned and said to Cullen, "Tommy, take a walk."

"What are you gonna do?" Cullen protested.

"Don't you get it? He *knew* he'd get caught! That's why he videotaped Eddie's murder. He thinks he's gonna get off!" Jordy yelled back.

"Don't stoop to his level," Cullen said.

Jordy tossed the car keys at Cullen and ordered, "Take the car. Get out of here."

"You can't kill him in cold blood, Jordy," Cullen protested.

Jordy tossed the car keys to Tommy, this time spitting his words, "Get in the car and go, Tommy."

Cullen hesitated, so Jordy bellowed, "Get outta here now! Get in that car and drive away! Do what I say or I'll kill you, too!"

There was no reasoning with him now, Cullen knew. It was out of his hands. He backed up nervously toward the redcap, got in, and drove away, leaving Jordy and Emil alone in the darkness.

Jordy took out Eddie's pistol, the one Emil had stolen from him. He opened the cylinder; there were two bullets inside. He snapped the cylinder shut and tucked the gun into Emil's belt. Still training his own gun on Emil, Jordy circled around to face him, like two desperados facing off on the dusty streets in an old Western movie. It would be a fair fight, not merely an execution. He unlocked Emil's handcuffs and tossed them into the street. Still holding his gun on Emil, he circled around to face him.

"Get your hands up!" Jordy cried. "Get 'em up!"

He shoved his gun into his waistband—the same place he put Emil's gun. He said, "You wanna be a real American? Go for your gun."

Emil raised his arms up, making it perfectly clear he had no intention of going for the gun in his belt.

Jordy said, "Pull the gun! You wanna be famous? Shoot *me*! You get more headlines and make more money!"

He grinned slyly and said to Jordy, "You can't

kill me. You're not a cop. Just fireman with a gun. I bet you never shot anyone in your life."

"You'll be my first," Jordy agreed, and pulled out his nine millimeter. He pressed the barrel right between Emil's eyes.

"Pull trigger," Emil said. "Do it. Oh, look— you're sweating." He grinned again, enraging Jordy. Emil taunted, "You don't have the balls."

Emil started singing a children's song in Czech, mocking Jordy, confident that he would never squeeze the trigger.

Jordy moved in closer. It was now or never—he could hear sirens wailing in the distance. He cocked the pistol and put it to Emil's temple. The cunning little Czech never even blinked. Jordy's breathing became harder; sweat rolled down his face. Pulling the trigger was murder, pure and simple. It flew in the face of everything he believed in.

"Where's your partner?" Jordy asked him.

"The Sheraton! On Broadway," Emil said. "Room two-ten. Go get Oleg. *He'll* kill you!"

A dozen cop cars, blue lights flashing, sirens blaring, cascaded down 130th Street. The lead car slammed to a halt. Leon Jackson bolted from it and came running, along with Tommy Cullen, who seemed greatly relieved that Jordy hadn't gone through with slaughtering Emil—at least not yet.

"Gimme your gun, Jordy," Leon said. "We all want him dead, but you can't do it this way."

Emil was grinning. Jordy lost it—he slammed Emil in the face, knocking him down. It felt better, but only a little. He jumped into his car and sped off.

The waiter's name was Zokie Mokomu, and he'd been in America less than six months. He'd been working the room-service beat at the Sheraton exactly three nights, though this was the first time he'd had a crazy-looking white man point a gun at his back as he wheeled his room-service cart down the hallway. On the cart was an ice bucket with a magnum bottle of champagne in it, and three glasses.

"Do you really need me for this?" Zokie asked Jordy.

Walking two inches behind him, Jordy said, "Keep your goddamn mouth shut. Don't screw this up."

They reached Oleg's room. The waiter, per Jordy's instructions, knocked on the door as Jordy flattened himself against the wall. Behind the door, a woman's voice asked, "Who's there?"

"R-room s-service," Zokie stammered.

The door opened. A pretty petite blond hooker

opened the door a crack. She was clad only in a towel. "Come in," she said.

Jordy made his move. He shoved Zokie aside; the frightened Nigerian took off down the hall. Jordy pushed into the room and yanked the hooker out into the hallway. He motioned for her to make herself scarce. She did, with little prompting.

Emil and Oleg had gotten themselves a suite—living room and bedroom. Jordy made his way silently toward the bedroom and peered through the door, which was slightly ajar. Oleg was sitting on the edge of the bed in his underpants. Sitting next to him were two very naked prostitutes. Oleg had hooked the video camera up to the television set and was proudly displaying his footage of the fire at Daphne's apartment building.

"Look at that! See that shot? Seamless. No cuts," Oleg was saying proudly. He grew more excited, adding, "And look—look at that transition. That's filmmaking! Isn't it great?"

Jordy kicked open the door, gun raised, and announced, "Don't move!"

The big Russian grabbed his precious video camera, then quickly got one of the prostitutes into a headlock. As she screamed in terror, Oleg got the second hooker in another headlock and rushed at Jordy, using the girls as twin battering rams.

"Let 'em go!" Jordy hollered. Oleg obeyed, pushing the whores at Jordy and knocking him back into the living room. Jordy hit the couch and fell over ass backward as Oleg, still clad only in his skivvies, dashed out of the suite and into the hallway.

Jordy jumped up, ignoring the hooker's hysterical screams and chased Oleg through the fire exit and into the stairwell. Oleg burst through a side door and found himself in the middle of Broadway, colliding with a group of Japanese tourists. He tore off down Broadway, knocking over unsuspecting pedestrians. The sight of a half-naked man running down a crowded sidewalk was, even in New York, unusual.

Gun in hand, Jordy gave chase. Groups of tourists parted like the Red Sea as Jordy weaved his way through the masses. Oleg ran out into the middle of Seventh Avenue, darting in and out of traffic. A taxi driver slammed on his brakes to keep from hitting the mad Russian, setting off a chain reaction of cars rear-ending each other. Jordy leaped over a smashed yellow taxi, closing the gap on Oleg, who was, not surprisingly, videotaping his latest New York adventure.

"Stop that man!" Jordy shouted into the crowd. Oleg ran head-on into a uniformed cop, knocking him flat. As the cop tried to regain his footing, Oleg backhanded him and grabbed his revolver. He squeezed off a shot at Jordy, missing by a good two feet. The crowds of tourists started stampeding all over Seventh Avenue, trying to get out of the way. The cop tried to tackle Oleg by grabbing his ankles. Oleg plucked him off the sidewalk like he was a sack of flour and threw him into the windshield of a taxi.

Jordy, from his vantage point behind a mailbox, saw Oleg seek refuge in the lobby of the Criterion seven-screen movie theater. Jordy rushed through the door and saw the ticket taker flat on his back, dazed from one of Oleg's haymakers.

"Where is he?" Jordy asked. "Where'd he go?"

The ticket taker, a Middle Easterner, started babbling in Egyptian. Jordy said, "In English! Speak English!"

"There was a man in his underpants with a gun," the ticket taker responded, rubbing his jaw. "He went right in there." He pointed to a door that led to screen three, where 2 Days in the Valley was playing.

Jordy entered the theater and crouched down in the aisle, his gun drawn. The action on the screen was a night scene, which darkened the theater considerably. Jordy cut through a row of seats. The moviegoers saw his gun and scattered.

Two shots rang out. Jordy ducked, then realized the shots were coming from the screen. He heard a voice cry out, "Look! Over here!"

Jordy turned quickly. Oleg was up and firing at him—and trying to film Jordy's death with the video camera in the process. Jordy ducked again, then jumped up and tried to get a bead on Oleg. The crazy Russian was vaulting over the seats five rows ahead, leaping from one to the other, smashing the shoulders and heads of the unfortunate moviegoers who'd paid ten dollars apiece for the privilege. He turned and squeezed off a shot at Jordy, hitting one man in the audience in the throat.

Jordy managed to get a clean shot off but missed. On-screen, the bad guy was also blasting away, which added to the insanity inside the theater. Oleg bounded onto the stage in front of the movie screen, backlit by the light of the cunning film. He was now officially a part of the show. He grabbed a young Puerto Rican woman and yanked her clear off her feet. He held her up over his head like a half-naked Russian King Kong.

"I'm on top of the world, Ma!" he cried, mimicking Jimmy Cagney in *White Heat*. "Top of the world!"

Jordy hesitated firing off another shot for fear of hitting the young woman. In mortal terror she cried, "Somebody help me!"

"Frankly, my dear, I don't give a damn!" Oleg bellowed, and then heaved the woman into the crowd of fleeing moviegoers, knocking them over like bowling pins. Jordy aimed again as the theater lights came on, but by this time Oleg was gone. Jordy bounded up onto the platform and made his way backstage. He pushed through the fire door and came out onto Broadway.

Oleg had disappeared.

"Shit!" Jordy said.

THIRTEEN

"And the wild chase through Times Square ended with the suspect, Oleg Razgul, escaping. The fire department has identified the fire marshal involved in the failed pursuit as Jordan Warsaw . . ." came the special TV report from Times Square

The channel was changed to CNN. Peter Arnett was covering the same story. It was big news. "In a related matter, Mr. Slovak's attorney, Bruce Cutler—famous for handling sensational cases—claims his client is unfit to stand trial," Arnett stated.

Daphne Handlova sat in the tiny jail in the NYFD's holding cell in downtown Brooklyn. She was watching the television through the bars.

Peter Arnett went on. "In fact, Cutler claimed Mr. Slovak was not the alleged mastermind behind the murders. According to Cutler, Mr. Slovak was being directed by his partner, who threatened to kill him if he didn't follow Mr. Razgul's orders. Cutler told reporters today that Mr. Razgul did, in fact, stab his client."

The scene cut away to a shot of Bruce Cutler holding a press conference. "My client, Mr. Slovak, is a victim. What's happened is not his fault. Emil was under the influence of his partner. At the trial, you'll see that my client will be vindicated."

Daphne shook her head in amazement. Under the influence of his partner? Only in America.

He would go free, Daphne thought. And when he did, he would come for her. To kill her, if for no other reason than he liked it. Emil Slovak actually enjoyed killing people.

Bruce Cutler loved watching himself on television, especially if he was discussing a high-profile case. And Emil Slovak's was indeed a high-profile case, perhaps Cutler's biggest since the glory days of Gotti and the Gambino crime family. Now Cutler was sitting across a small table from Emil Slovak in an interview room inside Bellevue Hospital's mental observation unit. Bellevue was the place where crazy people were sent in New York City. The Magic Kingdom. The loony bin. The nuthatch. Bellevue was called all of these and more.

Emil was handcuffed. His ankle had been properly bandaged, and he was clad in regulation Belle-vue fashion—a green jumpsuit, slippers, and white socks.

"I brought you some letters," Cutler said. "It's really fan mail. Women mostly. One wants to buy you clothes. Another sent a check. Another *wants* a check."

Emil tittered. Americans embraced violence the way Catholics embraced their Pope. He asked Cutler, "You bring me the cigarettes?"

"Sure," Cutler answered. He shook a Parliament out of a pack, put it in Emil's mouth, and lit it for him. "Are they treating you all right?"

Emil didn't respond, just stared at him vacantly. He made Cutler nervous.

"I want to get the cuffs off, but there's a little bit of a problem," he said to Emil." Things out there are very negative right now. We got to change that around. Perception is very, very important. Perception is reality. But it's important that I get that message out. That's our only defense in this case."

Emil puffed away. When the ash got long, Cutler plucked the cigarette from Emil's lips, tipped the ash, and put the butt back between Emil's lips.

"You have to focus on three things," Cutler instructed his client. "Fear, delusions, and paranoia."

"I was all of those," Emil said.

"But you never appreciated the severity of it until now," Cutler said, already coaching him. It was never too soon to start, as experience in hundreds of courtrooms had taught him. "No question about that."

The little Czech prick was shrewd, Cutler knew. You could see it in his eyes, two black, lifeless orbs that belied a burning intelligence. Emil asked, "What about Oleg?"

"They're looking all over for him," Cutler answered. "Haven't found him. Maybe he went back to Europe."

"No," Emil said matter of factly. "He's here."

"Don't worry about him," Cutler advised. "Think about yourself."

"Okay," Emil said placidly, then asked anxiously, "What about my movie rights? Book rights?"

"I haven't really focused on that kind of thing," Cutler replied. If nothing else, Emil Slovak seemed to understand the culture of celebrity in America.

"What's your cut? How much?" Emil asked.

"I would say . . . half," Cutler said. "Half is fair."

"Thirty percent," Emil said flatly. "No more. Or I call another lawyer. This is the biggest case of your life. Don't try to negotiate—thirty percent. Say yes or no."

"This is not all about money, Emil," Cutler answered. "I need your trust in me."

"Okay. What else do you need?" Emil seemed to like that.

"I need to know about your background. I need to know about your upbringing. Why you're here."

"Give me another cigarette, please," Emil said. Cutler stuffed another cigarette in Emil's mouth and lit it.

Cutler said, "Tell me about yourself. What you did as a young boy . . . what your parents were like."

"My father always degraded me . . . killed my self-esteem," Emil said dejectedly. "And my mother was blind."

"Your mother was blind?"

"She went blind giving birth to me," Emil said. "She went to a black market doctor to induce me."

"Back in the Czech Republic?" Cutler asked.

"Yeah," Emil said. "Bad doctor gave her bad drugs which made her go blind. And my father blamed me for her blindness."

"Your father blamed you for your mother's blindness?"

"Yeah." Emil shrugged. "He hated me from the day I was born. Can you put the cigarette out?"

Cutler took the cigarette from Emil's lips and tamped it out.

"That's what he did to me," Emil said casually. "He put cigarettes out on me."

Cutler, ever the Brooklyn hardcase, was shocked. "Your father put cigarettes out on you?"

"Out on my back," Emil said. "When I was a small boy."

Cutler had struck pay dirt. "Can I see your back?"

"Help yourself," Emil said genially.

Cutler stood and came around behind Emil, pulling his shirt up. His bulldog jaw dropped about three inches when he saw it. Emil's back was covered with hideous purple welts from countless cigarette burns. Cutler had represented some pretty gnarly bastards in his day, but nothing prepared him for this. He recoiled in horror. At the same time he quickly estimated that each burn on Emil's back—and there were dozens—was worth about $100,000, give or take.

"Jesus," he said in a low voice.

"I'm abused," Emil said. "Don't you think?"

"This is not abuse. This is torture," Cutler said.

Deputy Chief Fire Marshal Declan Duffy sat behind his desk in his office at Fire Station 91 and looked at Jordy, his expression angry, with a little sorrow and pity tossed into the mix. The subpoena was clenched in Duffy's hand. His ruddy complexion was bordering on an angry purple. "The public doesn't have any idea what we do and now you're gonna define our image. This is gonna be our Rodney King!" he yelled.

"What was I supposed to do? The guy tried to mug me! I was gonna send a cop back—I just forgot," Jordy argued.

Duffy asked Jordy, "Forgot? You handcuffed a civilian to a fucking tree in Central Park!" Duffy threw back.

"Chief, I know I screwed up, all right?" Jordy said. "But it's not like this guy is just some innocent—"

Two fire marshals were watching through the blinds as the chief reamed Jordy. "Well, this guy is gonna end your career—and probably mine, too," Duffy shouted.

"End my career?" Jordy asked increduously.

Duffy said, "How are you going to fight this? Maybe if Oleg hadn't gotten away and you'd been on the front pages, as a fucking hero, this thing would be easier to fight. You'd have the good to weigh against the bad. It's unfortunate that I have to make decisions based upon your press coverage,

but there's nothing I can do. Gimme your shield,"
Duffy grumbled.

"But, Chief—over this?" Jordy pleaded.

"There's nothing to talk about," Duffy stated.
"Get a good lawyer. You're suspended until your
trial."

Jordy sighed in disgust, dying inside. He dropped
his shield, his handcuffs, his pager, and his gun on
Duffy's desk.

"I know you've got backup at home. Drop it off
here," Duffy said as he picked up Jordy's gun.

FOURTEEN

The saga of Emil Slovak, Oleg Razgul, and Eddie Flemming's murder would not go away. Follow-up front-page stories clogged the three daily newspapers and monopolized the local airwaves. Journalists were having a field day with this one—a much beloved murdered NYPD detective, not to mention a dead prostitute, a shoot-out in a movie theater, and several foot chases in Times Square made for first-rate copy. The staunchly right-wing *New York Post* wanted Emil and Oleg firmly in the electric chair; the moderate, leaning-to-left-wing *Daily News* was taking a wait-and-see attitude. The *New York Times* consulted a battery of legal scholars from universities and think tanks and, as usual, painted Emil Slovak as a victim of a repressive society who needed sympathy and understanding.

It didn't end there. The case roused feelings on

every hot-button topic from enforcing tougher im-migration standards to the proliferation of harmful trash TV shows—most notably tabloids like *Top Story* and its ilk.

Down at the Immigration and Naturalization Office in lower Manhattan, Jordy was talking with Bill Stern, a senior special agent with the INS. In the adjoining office, Daphne was conversing with a couple of young assistant U.S. attorneys.

"Look, what don't you understand?" Bill Stern was saying to Jordy. "We've got a good relationship with the Czechs—the State Department doesn't want to cause an incident."

"But the DA needs her as an eyewitness!" Jordy maintained.

"They've got her testimony on videotape," Stern explained. "And even if they do take her to court, immediately after she'll be extradicted. The Czechs want her back. She shot a cop! I mean, Christ, man, what if Emil Slovak and Oleg Razgul fled to the Czech Republic? How would you feel if the Czechs wouldn't give them back to us?"

Stern looked through the glass partition at Daphne. He turned to Jordy and lowered his voice, saying, "And just between us, I was married to a redhead. They're a jinx. Redheads are like cross-eyed priests. Stay away from 'em both."

Jordy gave him a look. Stern realized he'd probably crossed a line somewhere. He said, "You want to see her, go ahead."

Jordy went into the office where Daphne had been talking to the young assistant U.S. attorneys, who were leaving. Jordy sat down next to her.

"We're gonna fight the extradition," he said to her.

Daphne took Jordy's bandaged hand in hers. She said, "Forget about me. You have enough problems of your own."

"Do you really want me to forget about you?" he asked.

"I don't want to drag you down with me," she said.

"Daphne, I—" he started to say. Daphne touched a finger to his lips.

"Shhhh," she said. She leaned in and kissed him. She looked deeply into his eyes, trying to find a smile. She wasn't quite successful.

In front of the Federal Courthouse in downtown Manhattan, Nicolette Karas was trying to do her job, and was having a difficult time. It was only two weeks after Eddie's murder; her producer begged her to take some time off but she had refused. Despite the best efforts of her makeup man, she looked worn, tired, and frazzled. She'd lost weight, and she appeared hollow-eyed, generally unraveling every evening on the local news. She tried a dry run before the camera rolled.

She said, ". . . and today with his partner, who he blamed for the crimes, still at large, Emil Slovak will appear in court. His lawyer will argue that he is mentally unfit to stand trial. Eyewitness News has also learned that later this month, Jordy Warsaw will himself be appearing in court. He will be arraigned on charges of violating the civil rights of Zwangen . . . Zwangen . . ."

"Zwangendaba," whispered Spiros, her cameraman.

"Goddamn assholes everywhere," she snapped. "Zwangenbobby . . . Zwangendaba. I got it! I'll do it. Shit. Let's start again."

At that very moment, Jordy Warsaw sat on the worn couch in his apartment, drinking straight bourbon as he watched TV. He rubbed some salve on his burned hand; it was healing nicely. He was bleary-eyed and drunk for the simple reasons that he had no job, no Daphne, and he was being sued by a street thug with a name nobody could pronounce. Daphne was still in a holding cell in the Department of Immigration, pending her extradition back to her home country. The prospects of keeping her here didn't look promising at all.

Nicolette Karas was reporting from City Hall. Anger seeped through every word as she said, "Mr. Zwangendaba claims to be a direct descendant of the African king from whom he takes his name . . ."

Then a picture of Jordy flashed on the screen just as the phone rang. Jordy picked it up and said, "Hello?" He listened for a moment and said, "No comment."

He hung up, but the phone rang again. "No comment," he said curtly, and slammed it down again. Disgusted, he changed the channel in time to see Robert Hawkins's face. He was interviewing Mr. Zwangendaba in Central Park.

Someone had cleaned him up. Wearing a suit and tie, he was freshly shaved and barbered. He was standing in the exact spot where Jordy had handcuffed him to the tree. Good old fucking Robert Hawkins. Jordy made a mental note to rip him a third nostril at the first opportunity.

"He robbed you?" Hawkins asked him.

Obie Zwangendaba said solemnly into the *Top Story* camera, ". . . That's right. I just encountered him right here. I was just askin' for change, and he whips out this big gun and pushes me up against the tree, whereupon he takes my money and hand-cuffs me to it, leavin' me there all exposed . . ."

Whereupon? Jordy poured another slug of bourbon. Someone—Hawkins most likely, or Obie's lawyer—had coached him well.

Zwangendaba continued. "—pushed me all up in the tree, you know, handcuffs me."

Jordy's phone rang again. This time he didn't bother answering it. Instead, in a drunken rage, he ripped it from the wall and flung it as hard as he could through the open window, where it smashed into a hundred plastic pieces in the courtyard behind his apartment building.

Telephones were an overrated pain in the ass anyway.

Disgusted, Jordy switched the channel again. This time, a reporter was standing in front of the jail-house Downtown. A picture of Emil was patched in on the upper-right-hand corner of the screen. He was smiling, decked out in a white shirt and tie.

The reporter said, ". . . And WBAI has learned that Mr. Slovak won't have to worry about how he is going to pay for his defense. He has received movie offers and has been in conversations with numerous publishing houses concerning the rights to his life story . . ."

*   *   *

In a smoke-filled Irish pub on Third Avenue and Forty-ninth Street, the television was also tuned to *Top Story*. The regulars in Clancy's Bar started booing. They were blue collar, shot-and-a-beer types, workingmen from Queens and Brooklyn who thought Robert Hawkins and Obie Zwangendaba were both full of shit.

At the end of the bar, Oleg Razgul nursed a beer and watched the television. He was wearing a slightly ridiculous disguise: A New York Yankees cap, a cheap wig, and ratty black mustache that had twice fallen into his beer.

Oleg glared at the television, squeezing his beer glass. Hate and envy consumed him. Emil had always been smarter, and now he was going to get all the money and fame that Oleg wanted so badly.

Or maybe he wasn't so smart after all, Oleg thought.

I'm smart, too.

Jordy Warsaw wasn't going to be watching television anytime soon.

He'd smashed the screen with a Jack Daniel's bottle sometime during the eleven o'clock news the night before. He was tired of seeing his face plastered all over the tube. Before the sports came on, he kicked the Magnavox twenty-five inch set off the

TV stand, slaying the beast once and for all. Jordy had decided that it was people like Rosie O'Donnell and Oprah and Jerry Springer and Robert Hawkins who polluted the airwaves with their self-righteous drivel.

It was eight in the morning. Jordy stared at himself in the bathroom mirror. He was bleary-eyed and badly in need of a shave. Despite this, he was ready for what he knew had to be done. He slapped a clip into his own personal .38—the one Duffy had told him to drop off.

Dark thoughts were dancing in his head. He'd made his decision the night before: if the courts and the absurdly liberal laws of the land aimed to deny Eddie Flemming and Daphne Handlova the justice they so richly deserved, then Jordan Warsaw would set the record straight.

He finished dressing. He put on a pair of sunglasses to complete his wardrobe. Then he went down to the street and hailed a cab.

"Where to?" asked the cabbie in a Brooklyn accent thicker than a slab of delicatessen cheesecake.

"Battery Park," Jordy told him.

FIFTEEN

The ride downtown to Battery Park took twenty minutes from Jordy's apartment on the Upper West Side and cost forty-two dollars on the taxi's meter—they'd hit some serious Midtown traffic. He was wearing sunglasses. He transferred the .38 out of his ankle holster and put it in his coat pocket.

The cabbie, watching the scene across the way, said, "I can't believe this guy got off. Unbelievable!"

Jordy handed the cabby his last fifty dollars and said, "Whatever's left over, keep."

It was a big day. Emil Slovak was being transferred from the Downtown lockup to Rikers Island via a police ferryboat. A dozen police cars, their sirens wailing, pulled up in front of Battery Park. Bringing up the rear was a blue-and-white police van, no doubt containing the suspect. The media was also there in droves, rushing Emil and Cutler despite the NYPD's best efforts to hold them back.

Jordy hopped out of the cab—even at a distance, he could see Emil Slovak smiling for the cameras. Jordy's rage was reaching the boiling point—it was now or never.

He spotted Leon Jackson sitting on a park bench, looking forlorn, frustrated, and pissed off. Their eyes met. Leon called out to him, but Jordy ignored him, walking on and gripping the .38 tightly in his pocket.

Not far away, still looking like she'd been washed hard and left hanging to dry, Nicolette Karas and her cameraman, Spiros, were watching Hawkins and his crew. She shot him a look of utter contempt and disgust, which Hawkins saw but chose to ignore.

"He said he'd be here," Hawkins said to his crew. "Pick him up as he comes through the crowd. Do you hear me? For Chrissakes, don't miss this!"

Dozens of feet away, the police van came to a stop. Emil, handcuffed, was hustled out of the van. Bruce Cutler jolted from his car and dutifully took his place alongside Emil and the police escorts. The swarm of reporters and TV newspeople followed, firing questions at Emil and Cutler.

Cutler announced to the eager press, "My client was suffering from a major illness of a schizophrenic nature wherein during times of intense stress, as a result of paranoid and psychotic delusions, there was impairment of his ability to appreciate wrongfulness . . . This is a victory for the mentally ill!"

As the crowd moved along, Jordy moved with them, at a safe distance. His gaze never left Emil, and his hand was still clutching the .38 in his pocket. He saw Nicolette Karas and her cameraman jostling for a place in the mob of media people.

"Before Emil boards the police boat and heads for Rikers Island, where he will be checked into the psych ward, I want to say one last word to you all," Cutler went on. "As you know, Emil was coerced by Oleg Razgul into committing these murders, yet Oleg is still out on the street, a free man, filming gruesome murders. My client and I hope he is brought to justice in the near future."

Jordy passed by Robert Hawkins.

Jordy was close enough now to glare right at Emil. Despite the frantic efforts of the press to get his attention, Emil looked back at Jordy and smiled victoriously, gloating as if to say, *"I won. I beat the system—your system."*

Jordy lost it then and there. He screamed at Emil, "What the fuck are you looking at, you piece of shit?"

The crowd turned toward Jordy. Cutler piped up, motioning to Jordy, "Officers, you have to watch him! He has assaulted my client on previous occasions."

A couple of patrolmen blocked Jordy from getting any closer to Emil. Hawkins, Nicolette, and the rest of the camera crews were getting it all on tape. "This is it?" Jordy cried out. "This scumbag kills Eddie Flemming, and now he gets to spend the rest of his life in some country club nuthouse? What about the victims? What about the families? What about *their* rights?"

"Mr. Warsaw," Cutler answered, "I understand you don't agree, but this is the system, and this is the law."

Jordy tried to shove past the officers. He was just close enough to Emil to hear the little bastard mutter, "Be careful. I can kill you. I am insane."

Reporters started slamming Cutler with questions. He did his best to answer them in order. As Hawkins was instructing his cameraman to get a shot of the ferry, he felt someone tap him on the shoulder. Hawkins turned. Oleg, wearing his disguise and toting his video camera, was standing there. Hawkins recognized him immediately, though none of the other reporters appeared to.

Oleg said to Hawkins, "Emil knew exactly what he was doing. You watch this."

"All right," Hawkins said. It was scoop time.

Hawkins looked into the video camera's LCD screen. He saw the tape of Emil explaining to Eddie Flemming, right before Emil murdered him, ". . . in the hospital I say I am not crazy . . . and because of your double-jeopardy law, we can't be tried for the same crime twice. We come out rich, free, and famous!"

Hawkins knew the real thing when he saw it. He said to Oleg excitedly, "Can we make a deal for this?"

Oleg popped the tape out of the camera and handed it to Hawkins, saying, "It's free."

As Cutler answered one question after another, Robert Hawkins's voice rang out, cutting above the din of the crowd, "Bruce! What would you say to evidence that proves your client is not insane?" He held up the videotape. *"Top Story* has the truth right here—from Oleg Razgul himself!"

Oleg called to his former friend accusingly, "Emil, you knew what you were doing! It's all here in my movie!"

"Officers, there's your killer! Do your duty—arrest him!" Cutler cried out.

A dozen cops tried to get to Oleg, but a sea of

reporters, who turned their cameras and microphones on him, blocked their path. Oleg cried out, "I am not a killer! I am the director! Action!"

Oleg then pulled out a gun and aimed it directly at Emil, who grabbed Cutler by the arm and used him as a shield. Oleg fired, hitting Cutler in the belly. Cutler went down, clutching his stomach as he dropped to his knees.

Half a dozen news crews would capture all that followed, but at the time, events seemed to unfold in slow motion. As Cutler sank to the ground, Emil grabbed a pistol from one of the cops, swiveled, and rapid-fired at Oleg, hitting him twice in the chest, his blood spurting everywhere. Oleg toppled over and disappeared from view in the pushing throng.

People started screaming—it was Times Square all over again—and all hell broke loose. Like a coiled snake, Emil darted forward and grabbed the person closest to him, which just happened to be Nicolette Karas. Emil put his handcuffed arm around her throat and pointed the gun at her head.

"Let her go!" Jordy cried out. "Let her go!"

Jordy and ten cops pointed their guns at Emil. The local precinct captain, a man named McManus, was a trained hostage negotiator. "Drop the gun! Don't shoot!" he cried out.

"Tell him to put the gun down!" Emil screamed back at McManus. He was more afraid of Jordy than of the cops.

"Hold your fire," McManus ordered. "Do not fire your weapons!" He said to Emil in a calmer voice, "Nobody's gonna fire anything, okay?"

It was a classic Mexican standoff. McManus tried to keep everything cool, calm, and collected—no easy feat given the situation. "Hold my line!" he called to his men.

"Let her go," Jordy said to Emil.

"Tell him to put the gun down!" Emil said to McManus. His eyes were that of a man gone mad with defiant rage at losing control of the game; there was little doubt he'd kill Nicolette.

"All right, all right," McManus said coolly, trying to stay on top of a situation that at that moment had the potential to turn into a bloodbath. He'd seen it happen before.

"Shoot him!" Nicolette wailed. "Take that shot, Jordy!"

"Nobody's gonna fire," McManus called out.

"Stay back!" Emil cried.

"Nobody's gonna fire, all right?" McManus assured Emil. He said to his troops, "Everybody stay back. Do not fire any weapons. Lower your weapons."

Nicolette kept exacerbating the predicament by insisting on crying out, "Shoot him!"

McManus wanted to shoot her himself. Instead, he ordered his men, "Lower those weapons now! Lower 'em!"

The cops lowered their guns—reluctantly. Each one wanted his own chance to plug the bastard who'd killed Eddie Flemming. Jordy, however, did not lower his .38. He was a fire marshal, and therefore did not feel compelled to obey the precinct captain's order.

"If he doesn't lower his gun I'll fucking kill her!" Emill barked at McManus.

Jordy held his ground, aiming squarely at Emil's head. Emil was attempting to back away with Nicolette. The media people, most of whom had dived for the closest cover, were nonetheless continuing to catch every minute on film and tape.

As Emil dragged Nicolette through the parting crowd of cops, Jordy said, "Let her go."

"Shoot!" Nicolette wailed, not caring whether she lived or died. "Shoot him!"

"Shut up!" Emil ordered. "I'll surrender if he lowers his gun."

"No! No! Don't you let him surrender! Don't you let this piece of shit surrender!" Nicolette continued to urge Jordy.

"If you don't let me surrender, I kill her now!" Emil countered.

"I don't care," Nicolette said. "Don't let him surrender!"

Hawkins pushed his cameraman to the front of the action, trying to get the best footage. The other news teams were more than happy to oblige. The other cops had lowered their guns—Jordy held his ground. He aimed to finish this, one way or the other.

"Officer Warsaw, for the last time, lower your fucking weapon!" McManus commanded Jordy.

Jordy ignored him, struggling to get a clean shot at Emil without plugging Nicolette in the process. Adrenaline pumping, heart pounding, he could not seem to get off one solid shot. Suddenly he lowered his .38 and just turned away. McManus relaxed until Emil pushed the envelope a little too far—he started laughing.

"No! No! Take that shot, Jordy," Nicolette pleaded again.

"Okay, he's lowering his gun," McManus said to Emil. "You don't have to shoot her."

Emil raised his arms to release Nicolette. When Jordy saw for certain that she was safely out of the picture, he spun around, aimed and fired, hitting Emil in the leg—just as Eddie Flemming had shot

Emil as he fled into Central Park. Nicolette fell straight into the arms of Captain McManus. Emil gaped at Jordy, surprised that the fire marshal had the balls to shoot. He raised his own gun and aimed at Jordy. But before he could squeeze off a shot, Jordy fired again, hitting Emil in the shoulder. Emil still wouldn't go down—the little prick was tough.

Jordy seized the opportunity and emptied the clip into Emil's chest and abdomen. Emil was propelled backward, looking almost comical as his feet did a little dance before he slumped to the ground, dead.

Take that, scumbag, Jordy thought. He wouldn't be carving up any cops or hookers anytime soon.

Nicolette became hysterical. McManus, holding her tightly, said to her, "You're okay, you're okay. Don't look at him."

Hawkins, who'd bravely sought refuge behind his cameraman, found his voice. "Fuck! Did you get that?"

The cameraman nodded. Another shot rang out above the crowd. A cop called out, "Hey, Chief—he's still alive!"

Oleg, who was sprawled out on the ground, was still breathing, with his camera in hand. He was still making his movie—and he finally had the ending he needed.

Hawkins was the first one to reach him. He

leaned over Oleg, who handed him the video camera. Hawkins, to his credit, understood immediately. He aimed the camera on Oleg and started filming. Oleg said with great effort, "A film by . . . Oleg Razgul."

Oleg blinked a few times, then stopped breathing.

Beautiful, Hawkins thought.

Oleg's eyes popped wide open, apparently in the throes of death. Hawkins, along with the rest of the crowd, jumped back in horror. Oleg smiled, coughing in pain.

"How was that?" he asked Hawkins.

Hawkins answered, in awe, "That was great."

Oleg's head rolled to one side, and he promptly expired, this time for real. Talk about your money shots. The only things missing now were the closing credits and the swell of the London Philharmonic providing the music.

Nicolette, grateful that Eddie's murderers were history, ran over to Jordy and thanked him. Jordy put something in her hand, saying, "I thought you might want this."

It was Eddie's shield, the one he'd taken from Daphne's burning bathroom.

He turned and walked away through the crowd. Hawkins deftly stashed Oleg's video camera in his

sports jacket, then chased after Jordy, his cameraman following along.

"Jordy, do you feel up to making a statement?"
Hawkins asked.

Jordy debated the merits of knocking Hawkins's
teeth down his throat; no jury would convict him.
Instead, he answered simply, "No."

Hawkins snapped at his crew, "All right, forget
it. No statement. Cut the camera." Lowering his
voice, he said to Jordy, "Listen, I can help you. Take
a lesson from Eddie. The media can be a powerful
ally."

Jordy ignored him and continued walking away.

Behind him, he heard Robert Hawkins yell, "Hey!
Eddie was my friend. I'd like to be yours, too."

Jordy turned and faced Hawkins, taking a minute
to absorb Hawkins's words. Jordy paused to collect
himself, then quickly punched Hawkins in the jaw,
putting all his muscle into it. Hawkins fell flat on
his ass. The crowd of people in Battery Park gasped
in surprise. Some disapproved, but most of them
looked at Jordy with silent admiration.

Hawkins, somewhat dazed, looked up at Jordy,
blood trickling from his split lip. Jordy looked down
at him with utter contempt, then glanced over at
one of the cops on the security detail. The cop nodded at Jordy with a slight smile, understanding

completely. Neither he nor any of the other cops made a move to stop Jordy.

Jordy walked off into the city.

Hawkins's cameraman helped the newscaster off the ground. The cameraman asked, "Are you all right?"

"Yeah, yeah," replied Hawkins as he wiped the blood from his mouth on his cameraman's shirt. "All right, get a shot of him leaving. Then pan back to me."

The cameraman obeyed, filming Jordy walking off into the distance. Though Jordy didn't want the media attention, that decision was now being taken from him. As always, the media won.

As the cameraman panned back to the reporter, Hawkins cleared his throat and looked earnestly into the lens, annoucing, "We've just been speaking with Fire Marshal Jordan Warsaw. He is understandably overwhelmed with what just occurred here—the tragic end of a vicious psychopath, a man who attempted to manipulate the news media in pursuit of his own greed."

He paused for a second, looking into the lens meaningfully as the camera angle slowly widened. To anyone standing and watching the broadcast on Broadway and Forty-second Street, Hawkins's face seemed to fill the entire screen of the Jumbotron overlooking Times Square.

As hundreds of New Yorkers watched, Hawkins continued. "We at *Top Story* will never allow ourselves to be used in this way. Our goal is to bring you the news in all its complexity. Truth was the real hero today, and we are proud to have brought it to you—exclusively on *Top Story*. This is Robert Hawkins. Good night."

Hawkins signed off, indeed giving the media the last word. Whether Jordy wanted it or not, he was now famous.

As famous as Eddie Flemming.

NEW LINE CINEMA PRESENTS AN INDUSTRY ENTERTAINMENT/TRIBECA PRODUCTION A JOHN HERZFELD PICTURE ROBERT DE NIRO EDWARD BURNS "FIFTEEN MINUTES" KELSEY GRAMMER AVERY BROOKS MELINA KANAKAREDES CASTING BY MINDY MARIN COSTUME DESIGNER APRIL FERRY MUSIC BY ANTHONY MARINELLI AND J. PETER ROBINSON EDITED BY STEVE COHEN, A.C.E. PRODUCTION DESIGNER MAYNE BERKE DIRECTOR OF PHOTOGRAPHY JEAN YVES ESCOFFIER PRODUCED BY KEITH ADDIS NICK WECHSLER PRODUCED BY DAVID BLOCKER JOHN HERZFELD EXECUTIVE PRODUCER CLAIRE RUDNICK POLSTEIN WRITTEN AND DIRECTED BY JOHN HERZFELD

Soundtrack Available on

NEW LINE CINEMA

AMERICA ONLINE KEYWORD: 15 Minutes   INTERNET KEYWORD: 15 Minutes

Novelization Available by
Penguin Putnam Publishing